HACKER EXPOSED

WHITE HAT SECURITY SERIES, BOOK 1

LINZI BAXTER

Hacker Exposed
White Hat Security Series, Book 1
Copyright © 2017 by Linzi Baxter
Cover Artist: Cassy Roop, Pink Ink Designs
Edited by: Jennifer Wadsworth, Red Adept Editing

All rights reserved. Except for use in any review, the reproduction or utilization of this work, in whole or in part, in any form by any electronic, mechanical, or other means now known or hereafter invented, is forbidden without permission of the author.

The unauthorized reproduction or distribution of this copyrighted work is illegal. Criminal copyright infringement (including infringement without monetary gain) is investigated by the FBI and is punishable by up to five years in federal prison and a fine of $250,000.

This is a work of fiction. Names, characters, businesses, places, events, and incidents are either the products of the author's imagination or used in a fictitious manner. Any resemblance to actual persons, living or dead, or actual events is purely coincidental.

ABOUT THIS BOOK

Bridget Boggs carries a lot of guilt over what happened to Alex Ross and his family. She had been good friends with the Ross boys until her greedy father lost part of the Ross family's savings in a pyramid scheme. He went to jail, and Bridget and her family changed their names and went into hiding.

Bridget imagines that Alex and his brothers feel just as betrayed as she does by her father's criminal acts. When she meets Alex again as a young hacker and the owner of a White Hat Security, he has something more important to talk about than her father's transgressions. A million dollars has been stolen from his company, and Alex needs Bridget's help to track down the culprit.

Alex has certainly grown up since they last met. The man looks like a Greek god, and Bridget can't help but be attracted to him. As she digs deeper into the theft from Ross Enterprises, Bridget doesn't need any more distractions. This is a more dangerous job than either Bridget or Alex expected. The thief is willing to go to incredible lengths to evade the police, and the two amateur sleuths may find themselves caught in the crossfire.

AUTHOR NOTE'S

White Hat Security Series

Hacker Exposed

Royal Hacker

Misunderstood Hacker

Undercover Hacker

Hacker Revelation

Hacker Christmas

Hacker Salvation - June 11, 2019

Immortal Dragon

The Dragon's Psychic - July 9, 2019

The Dragon's Human - 2019

Montana Gold (Brotherhood Kindle World)

Grayson's Angel

Noah's Love

Bryson's Treasure - 2019

A Flipping Love Story (Badge of Honor World)

Unlocking Dreams

Unlocking Hope - 2019

Siblings of the Underworld

Hell's Key (Part of the Shadows and Sorcery Box Set) May 28, 2019

Visit linzibaxter.com for more information and release dates.
Join Linzi Baxter Newsletter at Newsletter

1

ALEX

"The Citrix project is missing somewhere around a million dollars," Mr. Davis said. We were in my executive conference room, discussing each department's concerns. Missing money was a departmental concern, but it should have been brought to my attention as soon as it was discovered. Nobody should wait for a staff meeting to discuss something like that.

I was surprised because Mr. Davis had been working for Ross Enterprises as our CFO for twenty years and should have known better. I'd never cared for the guy. He was one of the last remaining employees from when my father ran Ross Enterprises. Charles Davis was in his early fifties and only around five foot five. He had one of those beer bellies that hung over his pants. Ever since I was a kid, I wondered if his hair was real or fake. I assumed, since it had never changed colors or appeared washed, it was fake. Over the past few months, I noticed he had become increasingly more anxious and uneasy whenever I came to his office unannounced.

The other executives started to shift in their seats. They

recognized I was about to lose it. But this was a blessing in disguise. Mr. Davis needed to be let go, and he had just given me a reason.

I tried to reply calmly. "I must have misunderstood you. Did you just say we are missing a million dollars like it doesn't fucking matter?" On second thought, it didn't come out all that calmly.

"I'm reading you the report the Citrix project account manager typed up," he said angrily.

Shannon King, the human resources manager, was shaking her head. I understood why she was doing it, but I didn't care. Mr. Davis was going to get fired. Charles should have been investigating how the money went missing, not relying on an account manager's report. Mr. Davis was lucky I was firing him instead of throwing him off the top of the building. Shannon should have been happy with me too.

"You're fired. Fred, please escort Mr. Davis out of the building." Fred was the top security officer at Ross Enterprises. He had been in the same unit as my brothers. When he needed a job after leaving the military, I'd hired him. The man was built, with muscles in places only body builders could have. Smart people didn't mess with him.

"You can't fire me!" Mr. Davis yelled as Fred escorted him out of the building.

I can fire anyone I want, I thought with bravado, while making a mental note to call the lawyers. They were going to be making extra money this week.

The remaining executives were all quiet. Shannon was writing down what I assumed were notes to save me from a lawsuit. I gave her job security.

"Does anyone remember who the account manager for the Citrix project is?" I asked.

Scott White replied, "Jessica Patterson was the account manager for that project. They have been looking to promote her to a larger role. I'm not sure if she is still working on the project."

Scott was the vice president of Ross Enterprises, and I relied on him for many of the everyday operations. He was in his early thirties. We attended the same school growing up, and later, we both went on to Harvard. When I took over the family business, neither my brothers nor my sister wanted to work at Ross Enterprises, so Scott became my number two.

"Sarah, please get Jessica up here now." I tried not to snap at her because she was my sixth assistant this year. I had stopped sleeping with them, which cut down the turnover somewhat.

"Yes, Mr. Ross."

This was going to be a mess. I hoped we could figure it out before the media got wind of it. A financial issue like this could affect our revenues. I needed it resolved before it got any larger.

"We will continue this meeting next week, unless any of you have more bombs to drop on my plate. If you learn anything else about this problem, let me know."

All the executives except Scott filed out of the conference room. Scott followed me back to my office. "About time you fired that asshole," he said with disgust in his voice.

"If you didn't like him, why didn't you do it sooner? You knew I didn't like the guy."

"It's hard to get rid of your father's employees," he said.

I had to agree. Despite my earlier bravado, I had a hard time getting rid of people that had worked for my father. Scott and I both respected my dad and his choices. But it was well past time to get rid of Charles Davis.

"What do you think about Jessica taking his position?" I asked Scott. Jessica had been offered a job at Ross Enterprises a few years back. She started as an intern and worked her way up, and she had done an outstanding job on a few projects.

"She's a little shy, but she knows her stuff. I expect this would be a good fit for her. But if you promote her, you can't fire her when she rattles off statistics," Scott said in mock warning. "I'm going to take a look at the project financials. If I find anything, I will notify you."

"I'm going to call Dad and get Ricky's number. In the meantime, let's keep this quiet and see if we can figure it out."

Scott nodded and left, heading back to his office across the hall from me.

"Mr. Ross, you needed me?" Jessica whispered. I hadn't noticed she had entered my office until she spoke. I realized I fired people all the time, and my employees were convinced I was an ass, but if they did their jobs, I didn't terminate them. Though, sometimes I did fire people for little reason. If they invaded my personal space, they would likely be looking for a new job.

Jessica was in her late twenties or early thirties. She had long chestnut-brown hair and always wore clothes too big for her. She was on the short side, perhaps around five foot three. When I looked at her, she appeared close to peeing her too-big gray slacks.

I didn't have time for timid people. I needed competent employees. So I decided to see if Jessica was ready for this promotion with a little test. If she didn't work out, I would move her back to her current role. "Can you explain the report you gave Mr. Davis?"

"I noticed the financial sheets hadn't lined up for the

last few months. I reported the issue to Mr. Davis, but he ignored me. I started an investigation to find the missing money and discover how much was missing. I put together another report and gave it to Mr. Davis." She handed me the report. It was well composed, and she had more confidence once she started to discuss her work.

"I believe we should create a fraud hotline," Jessica said. "I read an article where forty-two percent of fraud cases were turned in on an internal hotline. Only three percent of fraud cases were caught by an outside agency." Jessica proceeded to list a few more statistics. Based on her explanation, she was convinced someone had gotten into our IT systems and stolen the money.

"I will take that into consideration. You're being promoted to CFO. Get with human resources in reference to your promotion. I want you in my office tomorrow morning with an update. You can go now." The expression of surprise on Jessica's face as she left my office almost made me laugh.

"Sarah, can you get my father on the phone?"

I walked toward my desk, waiting for the call to come through. Looking out the window, I started to realize how empty my life felt. I worked sixty-hour weeks. I didn't spend much time with my family, but I spent way too much time with Scott at the bars. Perhaps it was time to start settling down and stop acting like a playboy. That way, I might also keep more female employees. I was so deep in reflection, I almost missed Sarah calling my name.

"Mr. Ross, your father is on line one," she said through the intercom.

"Hello, Father."

My dad had started with nothing and turned himself into a billionaire. When he retired, I took over Ross Enterprises. We all had the option to work for the family business or start our own company. The twins, Asher and Antonio, opened a security firm after retiring from the military. Their company tried to hire down-on-their-luck, ex-military employees. Asher and Antonio's firm had been doing extremely well for the last two years.

Aaron was a movie star. He had wanted to be a movie star his whole life. He had used his own talent to make it in the industry and didn't rely on his name at all. For the past three years, Aaron had been nominated for an Oscar. Last year, he finally won his first one.

Ever since we were kids, we knew Allison would become a doctor. She loved to help anyone when they were hurt. Two years ago, she did her first fieldwork for Doctors Without Borders. Now, we only saw her a couple times a year. She would visit briefly then head back out to her next location.

My dad chuckled in his deep baritone voice. He knew whenever I called him "Father," I needed something. "Hello, son. It's so good to hear from you. I know this isn't a personal call, since you never call to chat and never call from work. So what's going on?" One thing I loved about my father was that he always got right to the point.

"Do you still have Ricky's number?" Ricky was who Dad consulted when he needed to locate something awry in IT. If our system had been compromised, I didn't have faith that the current IT staff could locate the problem. "We found some discrepancies with the Citrix project. The account manager thinks we've been compromised. I need someone to look at the digital footprint." Whatever a digital footprint was. Hopefully, Ricky would be able to find a breach.

There was a long pause on the line. I looked at the phone to make sure we hadn't been disconnected.

"Ricky retired, but I have a new individual you can call," he said, a hint of delight in his voice. "I'll see if this person can meet us tonight at our usual restaurant around eight o'clock."

"I'll see you there, Father." I didn't know what he was thinking, and I didn't have time to worry about ulterior motives. That could wait until later. Right now, I needed to work on the new mall project.

2

MARTHA ROSS

"Martha, where are you?" Alexander Sr. bellowed.

Some days, my husband didn't understand how loud his voice was. We lived in a ten-thousand-square-foot home, which Alexander had built for me. After all these years of being married to him, I still couldn't believe the wealth we had.

"Darling, you don't need to yell. I'm right here."

He walked into the room and wrapped his arms around me. Whenever he held me, I forgot everything except him. We might've been together for thirty-two years, but I still melted in his arms.

"I have wonderful news."

"Okay, what is this great news?" I asked with a sigh as he pulled me in tighter.

"Someone stole a million dollars from Ross Enterprises."

I was stunned. I waited for the punch line, intrigued and a little worried. My husband hadn't been this excited since the last time he worked a large merger. After a moment, I replied. "Can you please explain why this is good news? Last time I checked, losing money wasn't good."

Energy was vibrating off him, and I could see the wheels turning in his brain. "Alex believes his company was compromised digitally. I found the perfect person to investigate the intrusion."

"What do you mean you found the perfect person to investigate the intrusion?" Then his words hit me, and all I could do was groan. "Please tell me you are not trying to use this issue and his company to get Alex married."

"Of course that's what I'm doing. I want grandkids. Out of our four sons and one daughter, none of them have given me what I want. The person I found will be the perfect match for Alex and will give me grandkids."

I couldn't believe we were having this conversation. "Honey, how do you know anyone our son's age that would be a perfect match? I want grandkids also, but we need to let them do this on their own and find their true love, as we did."

"We were married when we were in our early twenties. Alexander is now in his thirties. I have waited long enough. Bridget Boggs has an IT firm with a specialty in finding digital something or others. I don't understand all the technology stuff."

I didn't recognize the name at all. "Okay, I'll bite. Who is Bridget Boggs?"

"She's the daughter of Samuel Highmore."

"We've been looking for Katherine Highmore and her two daughters for years. When did you find them?"

"Katherine now goes by Greta. I finally found her a few months back. Bridget has done well for herself and her family. She runs one of the best IT firms around, and we need her to look at the issue."

"That girl has been through so much. You are not going to play matchmaker with her and our playboy son. I will not have her being hurt."

"I will make sure she doesn't get hurt."

This was a bad idea, and I knew it. But I also loved that girl and felt guilty for not helping the family after the incident. We had looked for them for years. We wanted to help them. Their father was an evil man, but the girls had gotten the wrong end of the stick.

3

BRIDGET

"What the fuck is wrong with your hair?" I asked while staring dumbfounded at my assistant. Her hair was the same color as a basketball. I was pretty sure it was black yesterday.

Patty was good at her job, screening phone calls and keeping me on schedule. Was she the most appropriately dressed or well-behaved assistant? Probably not. But when it came to getting the job done, she was amazing. I looked down and noticed what she was wearing. I decided I needed another cup of coffee, this time with a little more kick.

I kept telling myself to stay calm and not yell. Patty cried easily. She wouldn't tell us the story of her past, but we'd hacked the police records. That gave us enough information to figure out her family was horrible. So we accepted her into our mishmash of screwups and people hiding from their past.

"Did you dye your hair orange on purpose?" I asked in a calm and collected manner. Well, in my head it sounded calm and collected. Who knew how it sounded coming out of my mouth?

In the past year, Patty had started to fit in by giving us shit right back when we gave it to her. She proved it with the next thing that came out of her mouth. "You don't have to be such a bitch. I wanted to dye my hair lighter, and *poof*, I got this. I kind of like it, so I'm going to give it a try."

I wasn't sure if I should write her up because of her snark or give her a raise for it, but I was leaning toward the raise. Since she was already mad at me for my first question, I figured I might as well find out why she was dressed like she was. "Is there a reason you thought hot pink would match that hair color?" I added a little sass to see if she would cuss at me again. But Patty didn't have time to reply because Sophie walked in.

Sophie didn't have a filter. She said things no matter how mean they were. "Did you actually do that to yourself on purpose?" Sophie asked, pointing at Patty's hair and trying, unsuccessfully, not to laugh.

At least I got credit for not laughing at her. Patty got mad and stormed out of my office. Sophie sat in the chair across from me, still laughing. Before she could ask about Patty, I held up my hand. "I don't know, and I don't want to know. What's going on today?"

Sophie's position with White Hat Security was Cyber Security Network Engineer. Her ability as a hacker was well known on the dark web under the name Phoenix. She recovered from laughing and gave me a rundown on open projects. Then she said, "There was a strange phone message this morning from a Mr. Ross. He wants to know if you'll have dinner with him tonight to discuss a project."

I didn't imagine anything could top Patty's hair and outfit today, but a call from Mr. Ross was certainly unexpected. I hadn't seen Mr. and Mrs. Ross since they had put my dad in jail.

I didn't blame Mr. Ross for what he did. My dad was corrupt. He stole money from them and a lot of other people. After Dad had gone to jail, my mom continued down a road of depression, and I had to come up with a way to support the family. At one time, we had millions of dollars. After the government raided our houses, we moved to the projects with what little money we had left.

I started White Hat Security at twenty, and six years later, we were doing well. I could pay for my mother's care, and we didn't talk about my dad. He was still in jail, where he deserved to be.

"Bridget, did you hear anything I said? Who is this person? You look like I just said someone came back from the dead."

"Did he say where to meet him?"

"He mentioned a restaurant. I'll listen to the message again to get the name. I do remember he said something about eight o'clock."

"Tell him I will be there. Alexander Ross is the person who put my dad in jail for embezzlement."

"Wow!" Sophie exclaimed. "You're saying the Ross family as in *the* Ross family? With the playboy sons and more money than God? Wait, did you say your dad's in jail? I thought your dad was dead or a deadbeat, and that's why you guys never talked about him. We've been friends for years, so why am I only hearing this now?"

After my dad had embezzled millions, and my mom, my sister, and I moved to the projects, we changed our names and hid our past life. We haven't spoken to or associated with anyone from our past since. I worked hard to change our identities so no one would know who we were.

I still followed the Ross family to see how the boys and their sister were doing. I'd always had a crush on Alex, and I had been close with the twins, Antonio and Asher. We'd been inseparable and best friends throughout school.

"Hey, Bridget. Come back to earth and answer my fucking questions! Why didn't you tell me about your dad, and who is your dad?"

Sophie's yelling snapped me out of my thoughts. It was time to come clean. My past was a touchy subject, and Sophie didn't have any idea what was about to come out of my mouth. I met Sophie in tenth grade when I transferred to my new public school. She took me under her wing since we both loved computers, and we discovered we both loved to hack. I had told her we moved from another state and were starting over. Now it was time to explain the truth about my past. She was going to be pissed.

"My father's name is Samuel Highmore." I said it so faintly, I wasn't sure she heard me.

She was quiet for a good five minutes before she started to yell at me. "You're Samuel Highmore's daughter? That family was one of the wealthiest in the country. They had houses all over the world. Their kids went to private schools and had everything!" She looked a little pissed—okay, maybe outraged. If this were a cartoon, she'd have had red smoke coming out of her ears.

"I changed my family's identity after the incident. Mom's name was Katherine, Cassandra's name was Elizabeth, and my name was Claire," I said. "We didn't want the stigma of what my dad did to follow us, so we started a new life." Talking about my past always made me sad for two reasons. The first was what my dad did to all those people. The second was all the friends I had lost.

"I have been your friend for years. Why didn't you tell me about this?"

"I didn't want anyone to know who we were. I gave up that life. I don't understand how Mr. Ross found me. Our identities were buried extremely well. I did it myself. I'm taking this meeting to see how he found us and what he needs. I know what he did tore my family apart, but at least he took my dad down."

"Fine. Take the meeting. When I get to my office, I'll send you the name of the restaurant. But we are going to talk about this again later. I want to know what life was like back then and details about all the rich people. My best friend was famous at one time and friends with the Ross family!" Sophie got up and walked out before I could even respond. I had a lot to consider before this meeting.

4

BRIDGET

"I'm here to see Mr. Ross," I said to the maître d'. The local Italian restaurant was busy for a Monday night.

As the waitress led me to the table, I started to feel sick. My world was getting turned upside down. The new life I had created for my family wasn't supposed to collide with people from the past. The closer I got to the table, the more I started to sweat. Great. I was about to meet a client, and now I had sweaty armpits. At least I remembered to put on deodorant this morning. Or I hoped I had. There was no time to check.

"It's so good to see you, Claire. I'm sorry, I mean Bridget." Mr. Ross stood and swept me into the biggest hug. His smell and voice alone brought back so many memories that my eyes started to leak. I hadn't actually cried since my dad betrayed us, so my eyes were just leaking.

Mr. Ross pulled back and looked down at me with ocean-blue eyes. I had to look up because he was over six feet tall, and I noticed his hair was short with a dusting of salt and pepper. It looked like his eyes might start to leak, too, when he cleared his throat and asked me to have a seat.

"It's been way too long, Bridget. We've missed you." It seemed like he was trying to convey more than what he said.

I needed to figure out how our identities had been exposed. I had to fix that little issue so others couldn't find us. There were high-profile people who were still mad at my dad and, therefore, at my mom and us. "I wanted to ask how you..." I stopped talking when I saw a Greek god floating toward our table.

Okay, so it wasn't a Greek god, and he wasn't floating. Alex Ross was headed toward our table, walking with purpose. He was at least six foot five with short dark hair, the trademark ocean-blue eyes of the Ross family, and a body that would make any woman drool. Hopefully, I wasn't drooling, but my clit was beginning to throb. The man was wearing a beautiful suit, and I wondered what he would look like without it.

Next to me, I noticed Mr. Ross smirking, and I wasn't sure why. I needed to get my lady parts under control and focus.

"Good evening, Father," Alex said. The sound made my lady parts throb even more. Was it possible to have an orgasm from the sound of a voice? *Snap out of it, Bridget, and get your head in the game.* "Who is this lovely lady?"

"Hello, son. You remember Claire Highmore. She goes by Bridget Boggs now. Bridget owns a local IT firm called White Hat Security. I was hoping she could help you with your little money issue."

Alex was visibly shocked by the introduction. His eyes bugged out like a cartoon character's. Once he recovered, Alex put his charming smile back in place and aimed it at me, but I didn't know why. I was just a five-foot-four, glasses-wearing, curvy, black-haired IT nerd.

"Cla—uh, Bridget, it's great to see you. Have you met

up with the twins yet? I know they would love to see you again."

The meeting with the twins was the one I was most worried about. When we were younger, Asher was confused about certain feelings. I had hoped he would come out and tell people how he felt. But I followed the media over the years, and nothing had changed. Antonio would be angry at me for leaving and not asking his family for help.

"No, I haven't contacted Asher or Antonio yet. I'll need to talk to them before I start this project. I still don't know how Mr. Ross found me." I looked at Mr. Ross. He just smirked and popped a piece of bread in his mouth. It didn't look as though I'd be getting my answers this evening.

I heard Mr. Ross's phone chirp with a text. He checked it then said, "I'm so sorry, but I'm going to have to skip dinner. Martha needs me at home." Mr. Ross stood and kissed me on the cheek. "Bridget, please bring your mom and sister over for dinner this Sunday. Son, if you need anything, let me know." He walked away before I had a chance to respond.

"He didn't give me a choice about Sunday dinner. Hell, I haven't even told my mom and sister our cover is busted." I was having a mini panic attack when Alex broke through my thoughts.

"Dad has a way of getting what he wants," Alex said with a shrug.

"I guess that's why he's so successful in life. He doesn't give people the option of saying no," I said evenly. "We can get down to business so you can get back to your evening plans." The last part of that statement made my stomach churn with jealousy.

Alex gave me a pantie-wetting smile and said, "You have the job. Bring the contract over in the morning, and we can get started. The faster we find the person that did this, the better."

I was stunned. Didn't he want to make sure I knew what I was doing? "Don't get me wrong—I'm happy to take the job. But don't you want some references or to check out my firm's reputation?"

"No. My dad wouldn't have recommended you unless he was sure you could handle the job," Alex replied in a voice that didn't leave room for argument.

I bit the inside of my cheek, holding in the smile and the cheer. This would be one of White Hat Security's biggest private company contracts. I wanted to do a little dance, but it would have to wait until I got home. "I'll ask the waitress for the check, and we can leave. I assume you have plans tonight."

"No."

"No?" I replied, not sure what he was saying.

He smiled again. I had to wonder if that smile was attached to a nerve ending in my pants because it was making me so wet. I couldn't wait to get home, have a glass of wine, pull out "Bob," and take a nice bath. I would have some great mental images to take with me tonight.

"No, we are still having dinner, and I'm paying." Like his father, he didn't leave room for negotiation. *What is it with these men?* He waved the waiter over and ordered for us. If he wasn't so hot, I might have been angry. *It's 2017; I presume I can order for myself.* We would duke it out another night. Okay, that might have been wishful thinking.

"How are the twins?" I asked. I missed them so much. We should have figured out a different way to cope back then, but Mom was getting tormented by the media. We thought changing our identities was for the best.

"Asher is still quiet, and Antonio is still arrogant," Alex

replied. "They opened a security company after they got out of the military."

I might have been the only person who knew the reason Asher was quiet. He wasn't living the life he wanted. I thought I might have an idea about how to help him. And Antonio had always been an arrogant prick to everyone but me.

"So, do you have a boyfriend?" Alex asked. "I notice you don't wear a ring, so you must not be married." Out of all the questions Alex could have asked, I didn't expect he'd ask about my relationship status.

"No, I'm single. I don't really have time to date. We're still trying to make White Hat Security successful."

His brow furrowed. "Do you need referrals? I have a lot of business associates who could use your help."

"No, Alex, we're good, but thank you. I work hard to keep us in the black." However, it felt nice to have someone else concerned about us.

We continued asking questions back and forth all through dinner. Alex told me about his brothers and sister and what they were doing currently. I explained a little about Mom and Cassandra. I didn't get into how we lived. I didn't want the Ross family to feel sad about what happened to us.

"Wow, am I stuffed! It's been years since I've eaten here. The twins used to take me here all the time. Nice to see the family still has its own table."

As I stood from my chair, Alex was right next to me. He smelled so good. I might have brushed against him and taken a sniff. He led me out of the restaurant with his hand on my lower back. My body got all tingly.

"Did you drive or take the subway?" he purred in my ear.

How did he get so close? Or do I keep scooting closer to him? I needed to get my body and mind in check. *Oh shit. He asked me a question. What was the question again?*

"I drove. I'll see you tomorrow." Alex started to lean in, but then the stupid valet asked for my ticket. *Did the asshole not see that the god had been about to kiss me?*

On the drive home, all I could think about was the kiss that had almost happened. But it was good that we didn't kiss. Alex was about to be a client, and he was also the biggest playboy in the family. Tonight, I would go home and bask in the memory of the Greek god who almost kissed me. Then tomorrow after work, I would stop by the hospital and tell Mom and Cass that our cover was blown.

Alex

Of all the people Dad could have picked to help with the missing money, he picked Claire. I was not expecting to see Claire again. When we were young, she was extremely attractive but off-limits because she was Asher and Antonio's close friend. As an adult, she was even more beautiful than I remembered.

Throughout dinner, I was mesmerized by how Bridget had provided for her family and made the best out of an unpleasant situation. It showed how strong and independent she was. I could feel myself becoming infatuated with her. I didn't care if she was Asher and Antonio's friend anymore. She was the perfect woman to start a family with. I had a feeling she might be what was missing in my life.

5

BRIDGET

When I got home, I noticed the lights were on. It looked like Sophie wasn't going to wait until tomorrow for the scoop.

It was like rapid fire when I walked in the door. She didn't even let me take off my jacket or put down my purse before she started in with a string of questions. "So how was dinner with the upper class tonight? Did you get any details about those hot boys of his? I like the two twins. I wonder if they would have a threesome."

"I had dinner with Mr. Ross and his son Alex. We got the contract. I'm heading over there at nine tomorrow morning. I will take this project on myself with the help of CJ. As for the twins, I'm pretty sure they don't have threesomes. I'm trying to figure out what I'm going to say to them. They were my closest friends growing up."

"Wait! Did you just say you were close friends with the twins? My dream guy, times two, was best friends with my best friend?"

"Stop yelling. I'm right here. If the twins don't hate me for what I did, I will introduce you. I think you'd like Antonio better. Maybe you could settle down with him." An expression of horror showed on Sophie's face, and it made me smile. "Something wrong with your face? You look constipated."

"I don't want to date anyone. I'm looking for a wham-bam-thank-you-ma'am, nothing more."

"One of these days, someone will steal your heart when you least expect it, and you will settle down." I tried saying it with a straight face, but I couldn't.

Patty and CJ walked into the house. I wasn't sure why we were having an employee meeting at my house this late at night, but I had a feeling Sophie invited them over so I could tell them all about dinner.

CJ and Sophie had been friends for years before I met them. Sophie introduced me to CJ when I started at their school. The three of us spent hours learning computer code and everything we could about the dark web. During our senior year of school, CJ's family kicked him out for being gay, and he came to live with Mom, Cass, and me. Since his love for technology was the same as Sophie's and mine, it was an automatic decision that he would work with us when I opened White Hat Security.

"What the fuck happened to your hair now?" I asked. Patty's hair was striped black and orange, and she was wearing a neon-green dress.

"I wanted a change. You said my hair looked like a basketball, so I had highlights added."

"I don't believe you understand what highlights are supposed to be." It was getting late, and I didn't want to drag out this impromptu meeting, so we would have to tackle the hair issue another day. "I need to talk to you guys about our new client."

My staff was like my second family. We all had bad

pasts we didn't talk about. Some of them were worse than others, but each of us had stories to tell.

"We already know you met with the Ross family tonight. Why else do you think we're here? That family is gorgeous, and we want to know when we get to work with them," CJ said. Okay, so they wanted info on the hot family. I didn't need to tell them about my past.

I saw Sophie narrow her eyes at me. She expected me to tell them the story. *Damn*. For a second, I thought I wouldn't have to. "CJ, I'm going to need you to hand your projects off to another employee. The Ross family hired us to see if we can discover how a million dollars went missing from one of their projects." We had another six employees that did the grunt work, but CJ, Patty, and Sophie were my right-hand people.

"That sounds like an easy job. Why do you need me? Are you getting too relaxed in your old age and don't know how to hack anymore?"

I might have to hack his home computer network tonight and mess with him for making that comment.

"I'm going to tell you a little backstory that needs to stay between us. Sophie already knows. I told her this morning. Now I'm telling you because the Ross family knows." I found it hard to tell my friends this story. I didn't want them to know what my father had done. It embarrassed me. "Have you heard of Samuel Highmore?"

CJ answered. "Yeah. He stole a bunch of money about ten years ago. Now he's in jail. Why are you bringing him up?"

"Did you know he had a wife and two kids?"

"Stop with the questions and tell me why you need me on this job. Which member of the Ross family are we helping?"

"I am Samuel Highmore's daughter," I said in a rush.

"Um, can you repeat the mash of words you just said really fast? It almost sounded like you said you were Samuel Highmore's daughter, which would be impossible. The Highmores were rich. I went to school with you and lived with your family for a few years. You were poor like Sophie and me."

"We were rich before the Ross family put my dad in jail. The government took all the money away when my father went to prison. I changed our identities."

CJ stared at me with a blank look. I wasn't sure if he was mad or hurt. "CJ, say something. Will you help me? I don't want to meet with the family alone. The other reason I need help is because of Antonio and Asher Ross. They were my best friends, and I just left them. I found out tonight the family tried to find us. I might run into them working on this project, and I need you as a buffer. Actually, I know I will run into them on this project."

"Okay."

"Just okay? You find this out, and you don't say anything else? Are you mad at me for keeping this secret?"

"I'm not mad. Hurt, yes, but I would do anything for you, so I said okay. What time are we going to go over? I can't wait to look at Alex all day."

I saw red at the mention of Alex. I'm not sure where the feeling came from, and right now wasn't the time to figure it out unless I wanted my friends' opinions, and at the moment, I didn't want that. I wanted my friends to leave so I could take a bath and have a glass of wine.

"No, you will not be staring at Alex. I want you to work with Asher and Antonio," I snapped in reply then winced, hoping they didn't notice.

"Wait, do you have a thing for Alex? The twins are even

better. If one of the twins were gay, I'd be on cloud nine." Oh, if CJ only knew. Maybe they would hit it off.

I looked over at Patty, who looked like a deer caught in headlights. "Are you all right with keeping this a secret, Patty? I know you didn't grow up with us, but I consider you part of my second family and wanted you to know."

"I'm just shocked. Do we get to meet any of the family? I would love to meet Aaron." Now she had a dreamy look on her face.

"Okay, CJ, we need to be there at nine tomorrow morning." After discussing the agenda for the next day, I threatened to take away the team's Christmas bonuses if they didn't leave my house. Finally, it was time for a bath, a glass of wine, and my battery-operated device.

6

ALEX

The next morning, I woke up early, and for the first time in years, I was excited to go to work. I also needed a ride. My last driver sucked at getting me to meetings on time. I didn't tolerate being late. But I should probably consider finding replacements before I fired people.

Over on the counter, my phone started to ring, and it was just who I needed. "Hey, little bro, the man I was about to call. Can you swing by and pick me up? I have a job I need you to help me with."

I could hear Asher chuckle in the background. He knew how rashly I fired people and that I more than likely needed a ride. "How long did this one last before you fired him?"

I rolled my eyes and hung up. He would be here soon. Knowing Asher, he was already on his way to Ross Enterprises and probably only ten minutes away. I finished getting ready, grabbed a cup of coffee out of my state-of-the-art coffee machine, then headed down to the lobby of my condo building to wait for Asher.

I owned the building. It was one of the first projects I took on at Ross Enterprises. I bought the rundown apartment building and converted it into expensive condos. I transformed the top two floors of the fifty-story building into a penthouse.

"Thanks for the ride, Asher," I said, climbing into his black Range Rover. He didn't reply, but he held up his middle finger so I would know he heard me. I used the time in the car to figure out how to tell Asher about Bridget and White Hat Security helping us locate the missing money. He would be working with Bridget. I hoped Bridget coming back into our lives would bring my brother out of his shell. He seemed to be making the motions of life but not living to the fullest. He thought I didn't know his secret, but I knew everything about my siblings.

The trip to my office flew by. I asked Asher to come up so we could discuss the job I mentioned and so I could tell him about Bridget. The office was buzzing, and everyone was running around, doing their jobs. Nobody seemed to know about the missing money, and I wanted to keep it that way.

Sarah already had all the new documents laid out on my desk and coffee ready for me. She was going to work out, especially since I had my eye on Bridget. I figured it was time to settle down. If only my little nerd knew what was coming for her.

"You look like you have something on your mind," Asher said.

"I don't know how to tell you this. I hope you don't get angry," I said. Asher raised a brow but didn't say anything. "I hired Claire's IT firm to find out how we were compromised and to stop it from happening again."

"Sorry, man. You sleep with so many people, I can't keep up. Why would I care that you hired some chick?" He shrugged.

"Claire Highmore, your friend growing up. Well, she doesn't go by Claire anymore. She goes by Bridget."

Asher stared at me like I had two heads but didn't say anything. "I think I fucking heard you wrong, because if my brother had found Claire and didn't tell me, we would have a huge fucking issue." He looked like he was about to kill me. I believed Asher had a hiding spot to dispose of dead bodies. I wanted to sleep with Bridget, so I tried not to get killed.

"Dude, settle down. I didn't find her. Dad did. I didn't know until last night when he introduced her. Dad said she could help me with my current problem. Take your issues up with Dad, but please don't kill him. Mom would be upset." I tried adding the joke to lighten the mood. "You need to get your temper under control. Bridget is going to be here in a few, and you need to act friendly. Put that 'poor me' shit away and get your friend back. We need to gain her trust so she doesn't run again. Also, you and Antonio need to be at Sunday dinner this week. Dad is making her bring Greta and Cass. Those are the names Katherine and Elizabeth go by now."

Through the intercom, Sarah said, "Mr. Ross, there is a Bridget and CJ here to see you."

"Please let them in."

She looked stunning in her black dress. It fit her curves perfectly and made her breasts look so luscious. I needed to get my mind in the game before I embarrassed myself. The man walking behind her put his hand on her lower back, and I wanted to kill him. I wondered if Asher would show me the hiding spot for the dead bodies.

"Asher?" Her voice was so shaky, it sounded as though she were about to cry.

Asher walked up and engulfed her in a hug. It looked

like my little brother was getting a little wet-eyed too. I hadn't seen him express emotions in years. I felt confident Bridget was what Ash needed to help him figure out his life.

"I missed you, shorty," Asher whispered in Bridget's ear.

"I missed you too, Ash," Bridget said while holding Asher around the waist.

The tall Thor look-alike behind her cleared his throat. "Well, I love a reunion, but can we get to work? I want to go hack some criminal's computer and hand the info to the feds. Then we can pull up the camera feed, watch them get arrested, and post it online."

I could see Bridget start to chuckle and realized the guy was trying to lighten the mood for his boss. Now, that was a good employee. I wondered if I could steal him, though I wasn't sure I liked that he wanted to hack people's computers. I noticed the way he looked at Asher and realized I wouldn't have to kill him for touching Bridget. She was mine, though she didn't know it yet.

To her employee, Bridget replied, "I said no more hacking and posting to YouTube."

I had assumed the guy was joking. If this was a real thing, I wondered if I could find the channel.

"Damn, boss. You take the fun out of a job," he said with a smirk. He seemed to like working for Bridget.

"CJ, this is my friend Asher Ross, and that is Alex Ross. I want you to work with Asher to do in-depth checks on all the employees. You know the drill—hack and don't be found."

Asher replied, sounding annoyed, "What do you mean he is working with me? My security firm can pull all the employees' backgrounds. I have contacts who can pull extra background information if needed."

CJ and Bridget looked at each other and laughed.

"Asher, we are going to hack their checking accounts, home computers, phones, and any programs they use," Bridget said. "We also have the technology to hide those hacks so no one will know what happened."

"Come on, Asher. Why don't you show me this ex-military-staffed office of yours. If you're nice and buy me lunch, I won't hack your company," CJ said with all seriousness, and the two started walking out.

Suddenly, Asher turned around. "Are you going to be at Sunday dinner?" he asked Bridget, seeming scared she would disappear again. I would make sure she didn't, even if I had to put a tracking device on her.

Bridget nodded. "Yes, I'll be there."

Looking reassured, Asher left with CJ.

"I see what you did there," I said accusingly. "Did you do it for Asher, or did you do it to make yourself feel better?" I didn't want her playing games with my brother's heart.

Bridget looked thoughtful. She probably didn't think I knew about Asher and was trying to figure out what I meant by my question. "What? I need Ash's help. I don't know what you are talking about."

"Like fuck you don't. CJ is gay, and you're trying to set him up with my brother. Did you think I didn't know?"

She looked stunned. "He told his family?" she asked in a whisper. "I always pushed him to tell you or at least tell Antonio. I knew you guys would support him no matter what."

No matter how I broke this to her, she was going to feel bad for letting my brother's secret out. At least I was finally able to get some confirmation. Hopefully, he hit it off with CJ. I wasn't even gay, and I knew that guy was good-looking. He was like Thor in glasses.

"No, he hasn't told us," I said.

Bridget looked like she was about to pass out. "But... how did you know if he didn't tell you?"

I guided her over to the black leather couches that backed up to the floor-to-ceiling windows. My corner office was on the sixtieth floor. The view from the windows overlooked the Atlantic Ocean. While Bridget took a seat on the couch, I went to get her a glass of Scotch to help calm her down.

"I can't drink that in the middle of the day," Bridget said about my choice of drink. I chose to ignore her, put the Scotch in her hand, and told her to drink it.

"The family figured it out a long time ago. We are waiting for him to tell us." I told her as I sat next to her on the couch. I pulled her into a hug. *God, she feels right.* I looked down into those green eyes and started to lean into her. She smelled like fresh spring air, and I leaned in to feel those luscious lips...

The stupid intercom interrupted the moment. *I know I like my new assistant*, I thought, *but she might need to be fired anyway.*

"Jessica is here to see you," Sarah said through the speaker. "Do you want me to send her in?"

No, I don't want to be interrupted, my dick said, but my mind took over and pulled me away from Bridget. "We will be finishing this later," I said. I went to my desk before Bridget could reply. Her face looked so cute when she was stunned.

"Yes, send Jessica in," I replied with a shrug.

"Good morning, Mr. Ross." Jessica seemed to have grown a little more backbone overnight. I wondered if I should give her another test.

"What have you found?" I snapped. She needed to learn how to deal with me.

Bridget turned and narrowed her eyes at me. Was she going to stand up for one of my employees? While holding up air quotes and changing her voice, she said, "What Assbucket meant to say is, 'Good morning. This is Bridget Boggs with White Hat Security. I was wondering if you found any new information that might help us.'"

It took everything in me not to laugh. She was going to make my life more interesting. Jessica was also trying hard not to laugh. She held herself together pretty well. On the other hand, Bridget flat-out laughed. I would tie her up later and spank her for this turn of events.

"After further analysis, it seems to be happening in Ms. Hatcher's division," Jessica said. "The project is close to being done, so they are handing in the last of the billable hours. That's where I see the money missing, and it's looking to be more than a million. Did you know that sixty-four percent of embezzlement is done by women? Seventy-two percent of the time, it's someone in finance, bookkeeping, or accounting, and the average age of an embezzler is forty-three, according to *Equipment World*."

Jessica continued reciting more statistics until I told her to stop. Scott warned me about her fascination with statistics. I was a little shocked by her information. This was not good news. Losing that much money out of the project could cause the project to fail. Not to mention, Ms. Hatcher was one of my conquests. I hoped she wasn't doing something to get back at me.

"That is great news, Jessica," Bridget said happily. "You rock. We can take it from here. Also, please don't let anyone know I'm here. We want to keep it under wraps that an outside company is doing an investigation."

As Jessica left, I thought, *Okay, last time I checked, it was my business and my meeting.* "You want to tell me why we didn't get more details from Jessica before sending her out? Also, where do you get off calling me 'Assbucket' in front of my employees?" Bridget might have been cute, but she was starting to annoy me.

"I call it as I see it," Bridget said with a smile on her face. "And you were an ass. Jessica did nothing wrong, and you yelled at her. She gave me all the info I needed to get started. I don't want narrowed-down information. I want to look at the bigger picture. To start with, I will look at all the people that work on that project, including you. Also, what's up with the statistics lesson?"

Bridget pulled out her computer and started setting it up on the conference table in my office. She was taking over the place as though she owned it. Every minute I spent with her was making me like her so much more.

"Do you need me to call IT and get you a username and password?" I asked while picking up the phone.

"No, I already created one. I can't believe you use your mom's name for your password."

"How do you know my password?"

"I sent you a spam email last night. You clicked on it and entered your information. Thanks, by the way. Made my job easy." She turned and started typing on her computer. I guessed that was my cue to start working.

BRIDGET

"Can you hack my brother's computer or phone?" Alex swept his hands toward my laptop, like a push of a button made everything happen. "Didn't CJ say something about hacking computers? Can we do that? I have a few people we could check in on." So I guessed I could label Alex an unethical hacker.

It was time to teach Alex a lesson about hacking into people's things. I pulled up my notes from the research I did last night on Alex. In the notes, I had his iCloud password. Now I could look through the videos and pictures on his account. There was a video of him singing in the bathroom while getting ready. *Damn, is he hot, but a bad singer.*

"You mean like this video right here?" The shocked expression on his face and the stream of profanity that left his mouth made it seem as though he didn't like the feed I'd pulled. "You should check the video file on your phone every so often."

"You made your point. Now get rid of that and don't show anyone, or I will talk to CJ about blackmailing you back. Everyone has a price," Alex said. I knew CJ would never do anything against me, so I chose to ignore Alex and started installing programs and looking for the issues at hand.

A few hours later, I had a lead on who was behind the hack. I followed the money and caught the sneak who was using other employees' logins. I needed to get the identity to CJ so he could look into the guy more. We also needed to pull the video feed that corresponded with the login to verify what I thought was happening. Then we would have concrete evidence against the individual.

"Hey, Bridget. Are you ready to leave and grab a bite to eat? We can pick up where we left off tomorrow." Alex's voice knocked me out of my computer-induced trance. I looked up and noticed it was already seven o'clock.

"Wow, time flies when you get into the thick of things. I can't go to dinner tonight. I need to go see my mom." I also needed to get an update to CJ so he could pull the information together.

"I could take you to see your mom, and then we could get a late bite to eat," Alex said.

I wasn't sure how my family would take seeing him. "We can have dinner tomorrow after work. I need to explain to Mom and Cass that our identities have been discovered. It will be easier without you there. How about we meet back here tomorrow morning?"

Alex joined me on the elevator ride down. I texted CJ. *Can you look into the CFO? His logins don't look right.*

Did you get laid? CJ texted back.

No, I found some strange emails and logging on Mr. Davis's computer. It looks like the initial compromise was on his login. Can you pull the video feed along with the logins and see if they match?

I will take a look. Don't do anything I wouldn't do. He texted back immediately.

"Did they find anything?" Alex asked as we exited the elevator. I'm sure he wanted to know what was going on with his money.

"No, but they changed all the security passwords and added additional security protocols to the accounts that were compromised. I want CJ to look closer into Charles Davis's background. I think he is behind this whole thing."

7
―――
BRIDGET

At Saint Martin's hospital, the loudspeaker announced code blue, and the room number they stated was my mom's. I took off running toward her room and saw my sister outside. She had tears running down her face. The hospital staff wasn't letting her into the room.

"Cassandra, what's going on?" I asked in a panicked voice, trying to keep it together.

"I don't know. They won't let me in. The alarm was going off when I got here, and the nurses and doctors blocked me out." She looked as though she was about to vomit.

I didn't want to lose my mom. She was only in the hospital because of an odd rash. From the earlier discussion with her doctor, she was supposed to be getting out today.

Then I heard my mom's voice screaming at the doctors from inside the room. "Does it look like I'm having a heart attack? You dimwit, get those paddles away from me!"

I peeked my head into the room and asked, "Mom, are you okay? What's going on?" There had to be around six doctors and nurses in her room.

"These idiots think I'm having a heart attack and tried to kill me with those paddles. They didn't check to make sure I was okay before they decided to shock me." My mom is not the nicest person to the medical staff. When they wake her up or don't give her what she wants, she gets cruel.

Dr. Black was in the room. That man could give Alex a run for his money in the looks department. He'd been my mom's doctor for the past five years. "Bridget, it looks like one of your mother's heart rate monitors malfunctioned. It made it seem like she had a heart attack. Ms. Boggs, I'm sorry for the confusion." The doctor and nurses made a quick exit before my mother started to scream again.

"Okay, Dr. Black. Is there anything else we need to do?"

"No, she's good. I should be able to release her tomorrow." With a nod at me and Cass, Dr. Black left.

"Hey, Mom." I slowly walked into her room, trying not to get yelled at. After I told her about the Rosses, she'd probably yell at me anyway. "I need to talk to you and Cassandra about something." This was going to be a lot harder to talk about than I had originally anticipated.

"Out with it. It's not like we have all day."

"The Ross family found us," I whispered, hoping no one outside the room could hear me.

"So?" That was all she said, like I had just told her the sky was blue.

"Mom, that means our identities are out in the open. We can be found again."

"Listen, Bridget, it's been years. They aren't going to care about us anymore. Don't worry about it."

I noticed my sister fidgeting over on the other side of the room. She looked as though she wanted to say something. I started to get a strong feeling that I knew how the Ross family had found out our identities.

"Is there something you want to say, Cassandra?" I could tell by her body language that she was hiding something from me.

"I went to see Dad." Out of all the things she could have possibly said, that wasn't what I expected. Mom didn't look startled by the news, so she must have known.

"You guys didn't think to tell me you went to see the sperm donor?" I was pissed. I had worked hard to hide our identities and pay for Mom's living and Cassandra's school. Cassandra looked on the verge of tears, and I felt sorry for snapping, but I didn't understand.

"I wanted to know why he stole that money and made us pay for it. I wanted answers. You work so hard for us, and I appreciate that. I just wanted to know why." She was so young when we'd had to go into hiding, and she hadn't understood what was happening. For years, I felt sorry for the life she had lost.

From the look on her face, she had been hurt more by seeing him. "I take it he didn't answer your questions?"

She shook her head, and there was nothing else I could say. Cassandra didn't need to be hurt anymore, so I was going to drop the issue and make sure to keep my eyes open for potential problems.

"The Ross family wants us to come over for Sunday dinner. They didn't leave us an option, really, so we are all going." I noticed Cassandra still looked upset. "Cass, we have each other, and that is all we need. I will always love you. I'm not angry at you for what you did. You wanted answers. I do too, and someday we'll get them."

I stayed and talked with Mom and Cass about the Ross family for a while longer. Around nine, I decided it was time to go home. I kissed Mom and Cass goodbye and walked out to my beat-up blue Toyota Corolla that got me where I needed to go.

Still in a daze from today's events, I wasn't paying attention to my surroundings when I walked up to my front door. Someone grabbed me from behind.

8

ALEX

"Have you ever met that one woman, and then everything just clicks into place?" I asked Scott. After walking Bridget to her car, I came back up to my office. Scott left his office across the hall and decided to come have a Scotch with me.

"I came in here to have a drink and talk bullshit. When did we start having therapy sessions?" Scott replied.

"I'm serious. I think Bridget might be the one."

"Well, if you're into the short, nerdy type, go for it. I personally will never be ready to settle down. I like a different flavor every night."

"You've wanted to settle down in the past, if I remember correctly." Scott had been in a long-term relationship with his high school sweetheart. They'd split, and he had never wanted to talk about it. I figured one day he would.

"Been there, done that. Never again. So, when are you going to ask Bridget out?" I knew he was changing the subject because Rebecca was someone we never discussed.

"We're going to dinner after work tomorrow. I'm thinking about taking her some dinner tonight, though." *Damn, I have it bad.*

Scott was laughing at me because I wanted to see her again so soon. "Good luck, man. From the story you told me about how she reacted when you snapped at Jessica, I think she's going to make your life entertaining and keep you off the pedestal you put yourself on. I wish you both the best. See you tomorrow. I think I'm going to go look for a new flavor of the night." With that, Scott downed his glass of Aberfeldy and walked to the elevator door.

I needed to decide if I was going to wait until tomorrow to see Bridget or be a lovesick puppy and go tonight. I guessed she was still with her mom, so to burn some time and excess energy, I ran a few miles on the treadmill and caught up on the local news.

After my run, I decided I would go see Bridget. I picked up my phone to call my brother, knowing he would have Bridget's address. There was no way he worked with CJ all day and didn't get all the information he could on her. "Hey, big bro. What do you need?"

"I was wondering if you had Bridget's address." I was pacing back and forth, worrying he might ask questions.

"I had an inkling you would call for her number."

"What's that supposed to mean?"

"I will text you the address and phone number," he replied with a hint of laughter in his voice. I could hear CJ talking in the background.

"Oh, I forgot to tell you we figured out it was Mr. Davis who stole the money with the information Bridget sent us. We compared it to the video feed. The other information Bridget was able to pull makes it look like he's working with an outside source. We're trying to figure out who the outside source is. Also, she likes Chinese," Asher stated all at once.

"Is there a reason you waited to tell me now instead of

when you discovered the culprit?" I was livid. I really wished I could have fired my brother.

"Well, let me see... we only figured it out about a half an hour ago. Once I had concrete evidence, I reported the issue to my friend Lieutenant Malcolm at the police department. They put out a BOLO on him, and we were assisting the police to see if we could find a digital fingerprint. Mr. Davis knows we are on to him, so be careful. I'm surprised Dad hired and kept him with the record this guy has. We might need to look at rerunning all the employees' backgrounds. The strange part is he might be tied to Samuel Highmore, so Bridget might be in danger."

Apparently, I had jumped to conclusions when I thought they were slacking. Just in case Mr. Davis had figured out Bridget's team uncovered his part in the embezzlement, I needed to make sure Bridget was okay. It was possible I was just using it as an excuse to see Bridget, but I didn't care. "I'll go check on Bridget, and I'll bring her up to speed on the new information."

"Oh, and thanks a lot, fucker. You owe me a hundred bucks. I had a bet with CJ and Antonio that it would take a week before you asked for her information," he said, trying to hold back laughter. "CJ said you would be calling today, and Antonio told me you wouldn't ask."

"You guys need more work to do so you don't spend your time worrying about me." I didn't wait for him to reply. I knew he would send me the text with the information I needed.

On my way to Bridget's house, I decided she was mine, and I wasn't going to let anyone get in my way.

Once I pulled up to her white cottage-style home in a cookie-cutter neighborhood, I noticed the flowerpots in front were knocked over. Deep down in my gut, I knew something was wrong, so I called Ash.

"That was quick, bro. Did she turn you down already?"

Bridget was in trouble, and I didn't have time for my brother's jabs. "I got to Bridget's, and something feels off. You guys should head over. I'm going inside to see what's going on. Does CJ know if she has a hidden key?"

"Don't go in. Wait for Antonio, me, or the police. If things look real bad and you have to go in, there's a key under the planter by the driveway. Wait for us, though. We are on our way."

I knew I could count on my brothers, but I wasn't going to wait for them. If Bridget was in trouble, I was going to figure out how to protect her. Right as I made the decision to go in, I heard a blood-curdling scream come from inside the house.

I slowly walked up to the front of Bridget's home. I couldn't see inside because the drapes were drawn on the front window. But luckily, getting in was going to be the easy part of the night. The front door was open a crack. That was a win for team Alex.

I opened the door, trying not to make noise. *I need the twins to teach me some stealth moves*, I thought. *They would come in handy right about now*. I made a mental note to have them train me in self-defense, maybe even in shooting a gun.

Once I was in the house, I heard voices coming from the other room. I immediately knew who attacked Bridget. I didn't understand why he went after Bridget and not me, though. I'm the one who fired him. There was no way he could know I was interested in her. I had just figured it out myself ten minutes ago, hence the reason I was attempting to save her and not waiting for backup.

Not waiting for backup is really going to make my brothers furious, I thought. But I didn't like waiting. I just hoped we both made it out of this ordeal with no damage and a bad guy going to jail.

I texted Antonio that Mr. Davis was in Bridget's house and had her tied up. Then I turned off my phone, not waiting for a reply.

I slowly walked around the corner, hoping to assess the situation. I needed to get a better look at what was going on. Bridget saw me coming around the corner. I gave her a nod, hoping she would take that as a cue to keep Mr. Davis distracted so I could come up behind him and take him out. While I was looking for something to hit him with, I heard Bridget start to talk.

"I don't understand why you are doing this. Why are you going after me and not Alex? Alex's brothers found you out, so I don't understand why you're in my house or why you are trying to attack me."

I gave her an encouraging thumbs-up so she'd keep the lowlife distracted. I was curious why he'd come after her as well.

"Well, *Bridget*, I was only intending on taking out Alex and his family. But when I told my partner who was helping Alex, he said he wanted you taken out as well. Since you've hidden your family's identity so well, he's not been able to find you. But since your sister went to see him the other day, he's found a lot out about you guys. He wants me to get some information out of you, and then he said we can take care of you."

"You're saying my lowlife sperm donor put you up to this?" Bridget screamed. It looked as though she were close to going all Hulk. I needed to fix this before she got hurt.

Once we had the scumbag arrested, we could figure out what he was doing here.

I grabbed Bridget's laptop off the table so I could hit Davis over the head with it. Bridget shook her head at me. I didn't care about the computer. Hell, I could have bought her fifty computers. I just wanted her safe. But her actions made Mr. Davis take notice, and he turned around right as I was lifting the laptop above my head.

"Looks like the all-powerful Alex Ross is going to die today," Mr. Davis crowed, aiming a gun at me. I didn't know how I had put up with this jerk for all these years. He did well at hiding; I would give him that. But he was not going to make it past today if I had anything to say about it.

I might have been in over my head a tiny bit. He had a gun, and I had a laptop, and if I destroyed it, it looked as though Bridget would be mad. *I'm saving her life. She'll get over it, right?* I hoped she would. I didn't want to lose her over a stupid laptop.

"What do you want, Mr. Davis?" I asked. "We already figured out you stole the money."

"If it weren't for that bitch of an account manager, you wouldn't have found it. All she had to do was keep her mouth shut." *Okay, so at least I replaced this douche with a good employee.*

While he was caught up in telling Bridget how he had been skimming money off projects for years, I threw the laptop at his head. I'm not sure which distracted him more —the laptop hitting his face or the scream that came from Bridget's mouth. I knocked the gun out of his hands and hit him with an uppercut, hoping Bridget would get free of her restraints.

Going into a house where someone is being held hostage with no backup was probably not the best plan. I was a real estate mogul, not a ninja warrior like my brothers. Maybe I'd be a ninja warrior in-training soon, but right now they really needed to step on the gas and save me from this lunatic.

I struck out with another punch. Charles landed a few good punches right back. Those were going to hurt later. He got hold of a lamp and chucked the flowery base at my head. I ducked to miss the lamp, lost my footing, and ended up on the ground. While I was scrambling to get up, Charles got his gun back.

Davis pointed the gun at my head. *I hope he is a bad shot.* "Any last requests, Alex? If you had stayed away, I wouldn't have had to kill you." I heard a loud gunshot and wished I had spent at least one night with Bridget.

9

ALEX

I shut my eyes and waited for the pain to register, saying one last prayer and hoping Bridget would have a great life. Then I felt Charles fall on me. Asher had shot Charles in the arm and Antonio had hit him over the head, causing him to fall on me. Someone pulled Mr. Davis off and handcuffed him. I was covered in his blood.

"Hey, bro. Are you okay? Anything broken?" Asher asked while struggling with Charles. The twins had made it in time. I owed them big time. "What took you and Antonio so long to get to Bridget's?"

Antonio just made a grunting noise.

"No, I'm fine. I need to check on Bridget." I wanted to see her, but Asher wouldn't get out of my way.

"You need to clean your face and see a medic. CJ is with Bridget," he said.

I could hear Bridget panicking in the background and didn't care what I needed. I just wanted to get to her. I shoved my brother out of the way and went to Bridget.

I wrapped my arms around her and whispered in her

ear, trying to calm her down. "Hey, sweet girl. It's going to be okay. They got him. We're fine." I just kept rubbing her back, hoping to get through to her.

"He killed Alex. What am I going to do? I wasn't able to tell him how I felt. I wanted to kill him for destroying my laptop. I was supposed to kill him for that, not Mr. Davis!"

I tucked that bit of information away. I knew she was rambling because of shock, but that statement made me happy—the part about not telling me how she felt, not the part about wanting to kill me.

"Sweet girl, I'm right here. You heard one of the twin's guns. They shot Mr. Davis. They wounded him and knocked him out." Her eyes finally looked up and registered I was alive. She lost it and clung to me while the paramedics looked her over.

BRIDGET

It was too much to take in while the paramedics were around. I had almost died tonight because of my father. I needed to come up with a game plan to help protect my family from that nasty man. It seems he could still reach us, even from jail.

It was late by the time the twins and CJ left my house. I told CJ I wouldn't be in tomorrow, that he and Sophie needed to take care of the office. I was happy to see CJ and Asher hitting it off.

"Come on, sweet girl. Let's get you in the shower or bath." I didn't want Alex to leave, but I was just a curvy short girl, and he normally dated models. "Okay. Guess I'll see you Sunday."

The devilish smile that appeared on Alex's face was both sexy and scary. I didn't know how something so scary could also make my panties wet.

"I will see you at Sunday dinner, but I'm not going anywhere right now. You are going to shower. It will make you feel better. Then we are going to climb in bed, and I'm going to hold you all night."

I had no clue how I was going to sleep with a Greek god's arms around me all night, but I thought, *What the hell? I'm going to give it a try.* It might be the only time I would ever get him into my bed.

When I got out of the shower and went to my room, I saw that Alex must have used one of the other showers in the house. He was clean and standing next to the bed in his boxers. The Greek god with lights shining down on him from Olympus barely had any clothes on. That same god was standing in my bedroom, about to climb into my bed. *The doctor said I didn't have a brain injury, but damn. This can't be happening.*

I just stood there and stared. He had a nice six-pack that tapered down into a *v*. His hair was damp, and when he bent over to climb into bed, his butt muscles made me want to jump him.

"Are you just going to stare at me all night, or are you going to come to bed?"

Would it be bad if I wanted to just stare at you all night? I padded over to the bed and climbed in. I turned off the light and rolled over to my side. Alex spooned me, pulling me against his chest. It was so warm and hard. I snuggled in closer. I heard him groan behind me and couldn't resist wiggling a little more.

"Fuck. Me." Alex exhaled, and I could feel his warm breath on the back of my neck. Goose bumps rippled down my body. I closed my eyes, enjoying the feeling. Alex slowly pulled my shirt over my head, dragging his fingers across my sensitive skin and skimming over my tight nipples.

"You are even more beautiful than I could ever imagine," Alex said as he continued to drag his fingers up and down my spine. Once his fingers were nestled in the crack of my ass, I shifted in his hold, pushing my back against him. I could feel the heat radiating off Alex. He placed his hands on my hips and pulled me closer to him while continuing to run kisses along the nape of my neck.

Not being able to handle his slow touch anymore, I spun in Alex's arms. He had other ideas and twisted us so I was on my back and he was hovering over me. I could feel his hard length resting against my leg. I slowly grasped his dick with a firm hold and started to stroke.

"Easy, little one," he cautioned. "I want this to last. We need to be careful after the night you had."

"I don't want to go slow," I told Alex, reaching for his dick and stroking it again. I heard Alex groan, and he sucked on my tight nipples.

"Christ. If you keep that up, I'm not going to last long," Alex said breathily.

"I want to wrap my lips around your cock and suck on you," I told Alex.

"I don't think I can last with your lips around my cock. We'll have to do that another time," he said before moving down to suck on my clit.

"Oh, Alex," I said, panting. I reached for the top of his head so he knew not to stop. His tongue was everywhere. Every place it touched felt hot and smoldering. "Please," I whimpered, pleading, not sure if I wanted him to continue to lick me or finally fuck me.

"I knew you would taste exactly like that," Alex said.

He continued to slowly lick and suck my clit, blowing long puffs of air over my already needy area.

I was starting to lose control from his teasing and wanted him to fuck me. "Please fuck me, Alex," I said breathily.

"Not yet. I want you to come on my hands, first. Then, I want to feel you come on my dick."

Those words sent me over the edge. I had one of the most powerful orgasms I'd ever experienced. Alex continued to suck on my clit while pumping his fingers in and out of me. I couldn't remember the last time I was this wet.

"Fuck me," I demanded, holding my arms out to Alex.

He rose and kissed me passionately on the lips while sliding into me. Alex was so large it felt uncomfortable at first. He gave me a few seconds to adjust. Our bodies came together and fit perfectly.

This was better than any sex I'd ever had in my life. I didn't remember sex ever being that good. If it were, I'd have been doing it every day. It was the person I was with that made it so special. Alex and I fit together as though we were made for each other.

I wrapped my legs around his waist, encouraging him. "Faster, Alex. I'm about to come." I tightened my hold on his muscled back.

"So. Good," Alex groaned before his release.

We lay there for a few minutes, just listening to each other breathe and enjoying being wrapped in each other's arms.

"That was amazing," Alex said while moving onto his side and pulling me into his arms.

"I would have to agree with you," I said. After all the

excitement of the day and the spectacular lovemaking, I fell asleep in seconds. I felt so protected in Alex's arms.

10

BRIDGET

The next morning, I woke up to an empty bed. The afterglow of sex and thinking I might mean something to Alex had faded. I looked over to his side to see if he'd left me a note or any other sign he hadn't gone. Nothing.

I got out of my king-sized bed with a pink-patterned bedspread and brushed my teeth then headed toward the kitchen to get a cup of coffee. I heard sounds coming from down the hall. Turning the corner to head into the kitchen, I noticed two things. First, my kitchen looked small with Alex in it. Second, I thought I was falling in love. I know, I hadn't seen him in ten years, and it had only been one day.

"I was going to bring you breakfast in bed. Since you wrecked my surprise, come sit," Alex demanded.

"I thought you left," I said stupidly.

"Why would you think that?" Alex asked with a glare that warned me not to lie.

"I figured you didn't spend the night with women."

"Normally, I don't," Alex said. "You're different. What we had last night is different. You're the first woman I slept with and stayed with all night. I'm also planning to spend the day with you." His voice let me know there was no room for argument.

"Oh," was all I could say in response.

"What are your plans for the day?" he asked.

"I need to clean up the living room after the incident last night. Then I need to spend the day finding a new laptop." I let a little anger come through in my voice. Alex might have been great in bed, and he saved my life, but the man did wreck my laptop.

"Well, let's eat breakfast, have sex, clean up the living room, and then have sex. If we have time, we can get you a new laptop," Alex said with glee in his voice.

"You realize you wrecked one of the few things I care about in my whole house. You could have grabbed the lamp or anything else. Why my laptop?" I asked.

"Really, the idea you might get mad about me destroying your laptop didn't go through my head. But 'Oh shit, I don't want her to get hurt. Let's grab something close' did go through my head."

I understood where he was coming from, so I shut up and dug into the most delicious French toast I had ever had. *Damn! The man is good in bed, can cook, and is richer than almost everyone in the world.*

After breakfast, Alex had me on the kitchen counter. After another round of lovemaking, we worked on cleaning up the living room. It wasn't as bad as I remembered. We got everything back in order in about an hour.

I double-checked my laptop, and it was damaged beyond repair. Luckily, I had everything backed up to a second location. It was just a pain getting all the settings back to the way I liked them and reinstalling all the programs I used.

After cleaning up the living room, I headed to the bathroom to get ready. Alex said he would use the spare shower since I said there would be no more sex until I got a new laptop. He pouted. I ran and locked the door.

Once I was ready, I headed out to find Alex sitting in my living room, talking on the phone. He must have been talking to his brothers because they were discussing the money trail. Then I heard them talking about getting the money back into one of Alex's accounts.

While Alex talked to them, I worked on emails from the office. A government project came in that looked as though it would be taking up a lot of my time for the next week. I didn't know when I would get to see Alex again.

I wanted to enjoy my day with him because it was going to be a busy week. We would only get to see each other at night, if at all. It was possible I'd have to go to DC to help with the project on site.

"You ready to head to Best Buy?" Alex asked.

"No. We're headed somewhere else," I said, grabbing my keys.

We jumped into Alex's Tesla, and I gave him directions to Craig's computer store Technocure. I had been buying my computers from Craig for years. The man thought aliens were taking over the world, so he took extra caution putting all the new gadgets into computers. I figured that was why he built some of the best-encrypted laptops.

After picking up my new computer and introducing Alex to Craig, we headed out for lunch.

"If I promise never to hurt one of your computers again, do I ever have to go back there?" Alex asked while we were eating lunch. We had stopped at a local food truck to pick up tacos then headed to the beach to eat them and watch the waves and the people mingling.

By *there*, he meant Craig's shop. Craig wore tinfoil on

his head so the aliens couldn't hear his thoughts. When people he had never met walked into his shop, they needed to be tested. He ran a wand over them to make sure they didn't have devices in their bodies. He also made them answer a questionnaire before he would help them.

CJ, Sophie, and I had known Craig for years, so I got in with no problem. Alex had to jump through some hoops. It was quite entertaining.

"I think I would kill you if you broke another one of my laptops."

"Note taken. What are your plans for the week?" Alex asked.

"We just got a government contract this morning. I might have to head to DC tomorrow to meet with some people," I said.

"That sucks. When can I see you again?"

"I'll be back for Sunday dinner."

We spent the rest of the day and night in Alex's bed. The email I was dreading was in my inbox the next morning. I needed to head to DC and wouldn't be back until Saturday.

11

BRIDGET

The job in DC had more problems than I originally thought. Sophie and I didn't get back home until Sunday morning. Alex and I hadn't seen each other all week, and my body was craving his touch. But we had talked on the phone. We'd had some nice, heated discussions that made me want to jump on a plane. Sophie and I had worked late hours to get the project done so we could get back.

Cass and Mom were meeting at my house, and we were going to head to the Ross family's home together. The DC project took me away the day after I was threatened, so I hadn't had time to talk to Mom and Cass about it. CJ and Sophie were also meeting us at the Ross house for dinner.

"Hey, where are you at?" Cass yelled from the front door. She and Mom must have let themselves in. Ever since that night with Mr. Davis, I always double-checked to make sure I locked the doors. Alex and I had also been talking about taking classes from the twins. We both felt as though we needed to sharpen our defensive skills.

"In the living room. Why don't you guys come in for a

second so we can talk." I wanted to tell them the story now so we could formulate a game plan.

I walked over to give Mom and Cass hugs and asked them to sit down. "So, the night after I left the hospital, the man who was stealing money from the Ross family attacked me when I got home."

Mom and Cass both gasped and started asking questions at the same time in rapid fire. They needed to stop and listen to me. It was still a little frightening to talk about. I asked them to stop talking. Mom and Cass didn't listen. So I yelled at Mom and Cass to stop talking, and that got their attention.

I told them about how Mr. Davis was embezzling from the Ross family because they had put Dad in jail. After further digging this week, we'd discovered that Mr. Davis had been working with Dad for years. But we didn't know everything, and now Dad had lawyered up. He wouldn't talk to Asher when he'd tried to visit Dad in jail, and I wasn't ready to see the sperm donor, either.

Cass had tears running down her face. "I'm so sorry, Bridget. This is all my fault," she said between hiccups.

"Why do you think this is your fault? This is a scam Mr. Davis has been running on the Ross family for years." I knew why she thought it was her fault, but she had no clue Dad would try to have me killed.

"He wouldn't have come after you or known who you were if I hadn't gone to see him." Cass's crying was breaking my heart. She was my younger sister and meant everything to me. Mom looked as upset as Cass did, probably because neither of them had taken into consideration the ramifications of their actions.

"He was going after the Ross family. My company

figured out it was him doing the embezzling, so there was still a good chance he would have come after me."

"Are they going to do anything to your father for his part in this? I still can't believe he would come after his own kids. What is he going to do with more money in jail, anyway?" My mom looked as though she was about to go on a killing rampage. Since getting sick, she probably only weighed a hundred pounds. Taking someone down would be hard for her. At least she had some spunk. "I think I need to go see your father in jail. We are still technically married. I can try to get him to talk. When we have the information we need, I can cut off his balls and shove them down his throat. All I need is you or your sister to get me a sedative."

I couldn't believe my mom said all that with a straight face. That would have been priceless to see, but I didn't want my mom to go to jail. "Mom, we are not going to do anything to him. We need to make sure he stays in jail and away from us." The look in my mom's eyes said she was making other plans. Maybe I was going to have to keep an eye on my mom as well. I did not have time for that.

"Okay, since we are not going to make plans to castrate your dad, do you want to tell me how you and Alex are doing?" That was a quick change of topic. I wasn't sure I wanted to talk about either of those subjects, especially with my mom.

"You can talk to Alex when we get to the house and ask him how he is."

"I know you liked him when you were younger."

"Point to that statement is?"

"Are you two seeing each other?"

I tried to deflect her question. "The Ross family has been talking to us for two weeks. How did we go from talking to sleeping together?"

"I never asked if you were sleeping together. So it seems that you and Alex are dating. I like Alex. I hope it works out."

"Mom, there is nothing going on. Even if there were, look at me then look at the women he dates. It's a fling. Let's go see the family." Saying it was a fling made my heart hurt, but I knew it would never amount to anything. He needed a model with a good background to even out his life. I have neither of those.

"You are so much better than those women he dates. Let me talk to his parents. We will work this out."

"No, you will not try to marry me off. What is this, the 1800s?"

"I want grandkids, and neither of you are giving me what I want, so I need to step in and start the process."

"No, Mom, you don't. Let's go."

We all piled into my SUV and headed over to the Ross family house. I almost forgot to tell them about the other thing that was about to happen in their lives. I wasn't sure how they were going to take it.

"I talked with Asher early today. He and Antonio are hiring some bodyguards for both of you until we figure out what is going on with Dad. They don't have enough staff yet to use someone from their own payroll, but they have a friend, Sam, who has a well-established mercenary company. This company will be supplying the bodyguards. Asher said he would introduce us to Sam at dinner on Sunday."

"As long as they're hot, I don't care." My mom's reply stunned me into silence. She was in her late forties.

"I go to school, work, and home. I don't need a bodyguard," Cass replied.

"This is serious, you two. Mom, you will take a bodyguard even if he isn't hot. Cass, I don't care if you stay home. You're getting a bodyguard, or you will be with me at all times. I think you would prefer the first option."

They continued to talk about what they hoped for in a bodyguard. I informed them they could give Sam their lists and see what they get. I so hoped they wouldn't really make a list.

12

ALEX

I hadn't seen Bridget in a week, and I thought I was going to lose my mind. The last time I was this tied up over a woman was when Bridget disappeared from our lives. That wasn't going to happen again. I would put a tracking chip in her if I needed to.

Asher, Antonio, Dad, Aaron, and I were all in Dad's office, having a glass of Scotch, when Asher asked for everyone's attention. He had been fidgeting and acting strange all morning. I had a feeling I knew what was coming. Bridget had only been back in our family for a few days, and she was making an impact in the best possible way.

"I need to speak to you guys about something. This is hard to say, and it's not a choice. It's how I've felt my whole life," Asher said from his chair.

"Out with it, son. We don't have all day," Dad said with a chuckle. I think Dad knew what was coming too. Our whole family had been waiting for this day for years. I hoped Ash and CJ made it as a couple. They'd be good for each other.

"I would like to tell you guys that I'm gay and—"

"About time you told us," Dad said. "I thought you would never say it. Just because you're gay doesn't mean you don't have to give me grandkids. In fact, I expect them quicker since you will be able to adopt. Your mom is going to be so happy you finally told us."

Antonio gave Asher a slap on the back and told him he was glad he was finally telling the family.

"I don't understand. How did you know, and how long have you known?"

That was an easy answer. "Asher, we always knew. We wanted you to tell us. It wasn't our place to bring it up," I said, giving him a hug.

Mom walked into the room and asked, "What are you guys all hugging about? What did I miss?" Mom had a smile on her face and a twinkle in her eye. She already knew what had happened. We thought he might tell us today since CJ was coming over. It wouldn't have been fair to CJ to keep it a secret.

"Our son finally told us he's gay, Martha," Dad said way too loudly. I didn't think my father had a quiet setting. His voice was always loud, so the whole house and all the guests had heard. But it didn't matter because most people already knew Asher was gay and were waiting for him to admit it.

"About time you told us. I was starting to think you would never tell your mother." She walked over and hugged Asher around his waist, and there were tears in her eyes. She was trying not to cry. Hell, I was trying not to cry. This was an emotional day for all of us. I was happy he finally told us.

Sam walked into Dad's office. Sam owned the mercenary company we were going to use for the bodyguards for Bridget's family. He looked at all of us and said, "About time you came out of the closet. I was sick of throwing women at you when there were perfectly good men I could send your way."

Then CJ walked in the room with the biggest smile on his face. He walked over to Asher, put his arm around his waist, and said, "There will be no women or men being thrown his way. He is officially off the market."

Asher finally got his bearings back. "Antonio, you're not worried about our business? And what the fuck, Sam? How do you know I'm gay?"

Antonio spoke up first. "If our clients have any issue with you being gay, we don't need their business. Most of our friends already know, and all our military friends know. You didn't hide it as well as you thought."

Sam chimed in too, "Asher, I also own a BDSM club. Of course I knew. I can tell people's sexual preferences. I don't care what floats your boat, or your dick, as long as you're happy. From the way you look at the guy on your arm, I can tell you're happy. Best of luck to both of you."

I heard the chimes at the front door and knew my little nerd and her family had arrived. "If you'll excuse me, I have to go greet the rest of our guests." I heard Sam complain on my way out that no one had come to the door to greet him. He had been coming over to family dinners with the twins since they were in the military. My guess was he hadn't even rung the bell. He'd walked right into the house.

When I walked around the corner, Tabitha, the housekeeper, was letting Bridget, Cass, and their mom into the house. Bridget looked drop-dead gorgeous. I was going to have a hard time keeping my dick concealed with that outfit she was wearing.

Her black hair was down and reached the middle of her back. It was a nice contrast to the tight red dress that fitted against her luscious curves. Those black-rimmed glasses gave her the touch of nerd that threw me over the edge. I had slept with Victoria's Secret models, and it didn't compare to how I felt about Bridget.

She didn't know it, but she was coming home with me tonight. I couldn't wait to peel that dress off and see what she had on underneath.

I walked over and gave Bridget a hug then turned to her mom. She was looking better than I thought she might after having medical issues. I gave her a hug and let them know the family was in the study. I pointed the way to the study for Greta and Cassandra.

"Not so fast." I pulled Bridget over to the side. I had not seen her in a week, and it seemed like it had been longer.

I wrapped my arms around her, dropped my head, and kissed her like it might be the last time I would see her. Her arms wrapped around my neck and pulled me in tighter. We both were panting and so turned on that if one of us didn't stop this, we were going to have sex in my mother's entrance way. I was pretty sure my mom wouldn't appreciate that.

Slowly, I pulled away from her. We were both out of breath. Bridget's pupils were dilated. I could tell she was as turned on as I was. "Hey, baby girl, you ready to go see the family?" I wasn't. But if I were alone with her much longer, we would have an issue.

She was still dazed from the kiss as I led her toward my father's study. I could hear the men laughing and my mom crying in the study. As we walked in, I noticed my mother and Greta embracing each other with tears running down their faces.

My mother finally let Greta go. "You will never do that to our family again. I don't care what your low-life husband did. You were like family to me, and you left us. I understand why, but we would have helped you. I know you don't need help now because of your daughter. But we are here for you, and I expect you at our house every Sunday for dinner. Anytime you want to come over and talk, you're welcome to." My father had a hand wrapped around my mother's waist. He handed Mom his handkerchief. "I'm not sure why I'm crying. Today is one of the best days of my life. My son is letting his true self show, and our friends have been found."

I felt Bridget tense beside me. She wasn't here for the earlier talk about Ash. I leaned down and whispered in her ear, telling her Ash had come out to the family. I could see her relax and snuggle in closer to me. This felt so right.

My mom finally got her emotions under control when the staff walked in to say dinner was ready. We all went to the formal dining room. It was so full of joy and laughter. I couldn't remember the last time it was like this.

I could tell my mom wasn't going to let Greta get away this time. They were sitting next to each other, talking and laughing like no time had passed. Cassandra was talking with CJ and Asher, and there was joy on their faces. I wish our younger sister had been here. She would have enjoyed seeing the family this happy.

Greta tapped Sam on the sleeve to get his attention.

"I was informed you are supplying bodyguards to Cass and me?" She had a look of determination in her eyes. I hope she didn't give us too hard of a time about the bodyguards. They were needed.

"Yes, I have two of my best men for your bodyguards." I could see Sam was bracing for a fight. He would do anything for our family, which now included Bridget's.

Out of the corner of my eye, I could see Bridget shaking

her head at her mom. I wondered how their conversation about the bodyguards had gone.

Greta looked over at Bridget with a twinkle in her eye then turned back to Sam and said, "Bridget informed me about this earlier. I told her I wanted to know what they looked like and if they were hot enough. She told me to make a list of my requirements. Do you want that list now, or should I send it to you tomorrow?"

"Mom, I wasn't serious about the list. Take what you are given."

"Greta has a good point," my mom piped in. "She should have a say in what they look like. She is going to have to be around them all day, every day. At least she could have some eye candy."

Shocked, I looked over at Sam. He looked like a deer caught in the headlights. He recovered quickly, though.

"Well, Ms. Greta, I care more about your safety than arm candy. So you are going to take what I give you. I will also let you know they are all trained masters at my BDSM club. If you misbehave, you will be punished," Sam said with a straight face. I wasn't sure if he was stating the truth or pulling her leg.

Everyone laughed and went back to normal conversation about sports and what the ladies had been up to.

We hadn't seen Allison, the doctor, in a while. It seemed she stayed away longer and longer with each additional deployment she took on. I needed to check on her soon to see if she was doing okay.

Aaron, the movie star, had bags under his eyes. Aaron wasn't normally upset or stressed. He was usually happy and fun loving. I needed to pull him aside later to see what was wrong. If he didn't admit to anything, I would have someone look into it.

I was enjoying all the people around me and was deep in thought, so I didn't hear Antonio at first. He repeated, "Are you going to go to the trial for Mr. Davis?"

I didn't want to think about that. Bridget and CJ had been able to get the money back. I just wanted to make sure Mr. Davis would rot in jail. "I don't want to see that piece of shit. I'll send one of the lawyers to keep tabs on the trial. As long as he goes to jail for a long time, I don't care about anything else."

After dinner, I asked Cass if she would drive her mom home in Bridget's car. I wanted Bridget to spend the night with me. That way, she would have no excuse.

13

BRIDGET

The sexual tension in Alex's car was so strong, I didn't know how we were going to make it all the way back to the city. Six days away from Alex was too long. That was what scared me the most. The more I talked to him and the more I was around him, the deeper and deeper in love with him I fell.

Alex turned off the main road and headed down a dirt path I recognized. It was a back road to the guest lake cabin. We would spend hours up at the lake playing when we were kids.

"I can't wait any longer. I need you now," Alex said while climbing out of the Tesla.

I was right on his heels, feeling the same way. We headed up to the house. Alex unlocked the door in record time and led me toward the main bedroom. We were in such a hurry to get to the room, I wasn't even sure if we shut the front door.

"Let me see you," Alex purred in my ear as he ran his fingers down the side of my dress. "All I could think about all night was peeling this dress off your body, bending you over, and fucking you."

Alex sat on the bed, facing me, and asked me to strip for him. I ran my hands along the bottom of my dress. Very slowly, I worked it up to show him I wasn't wearing any underwear. He immediately dropped to his knees in front of me and started licking my already-wet pussy.

"Alex, I'm not going to last." I was wound up from not seeing him in a week. It only took a couple of pumps from Alex's fingers for me to come all over his hand and mouth. Alex continued to lick me until I came out of my orgasm-induced haze. Then he stood to pull my dress over my head and sucked on my tight nipples.

I dropped to my knees and unbuckled Alex's dress pants. Gently, I pulled out his dick and licked the underside while looking up at him. His head fell back as I continued to take him in my mouth. I enjoyed the power I had over Alex while sucking on him.

"Damn, you are good at that," Alex said. Then he pulled me to my feet and threw me on the bed.

"I wasn't done," I said, pouting.

"I don't want to come in your mouth. I want to come inside you."

Alex finished undressing, climbed on top of me, and made love to me. It was slow and meaningful. He hit me in all the right spots, and it didn't take long before I was ready to orgasm again.

"Alex, I'm about to come," I said breathily.

"Fuck, you're so good," Alex said in the crook of my neck.

I fell asleep with Alex still inside me. He woke me a couple times during the night. The next time was fast and rough, and after that, slow and sweet.

Too soon, the annoying Greek god in my bed said, "Time to get up."

"Really?" I grumbled.

"Yes. We are going out on the boat with CJ and Asher."

"When?" I was only asking one-word questions. It took less energy.

"Now," Alex said. Then he picked me up and carried me to the bathroom.

We spent the next hour in the shower. I didn't realize CJ and Asher were in the living room, waiting for us. When I walked out of the bedroom, CJ gave me a knowing look, and I turned red.

"You could have told me they were in the cabin," I grumbled at Alex. To CJ, I asked, "Wait, how did you know we were here?"

CJ's face turned as red as mine. I thought I knew why, but I wanted to hear it come out of their mouths.

"We didn't want to head back to the city, so we came to the cabin and slept in the other wing," Asher said.

This fucking cabin has wings? Since the cabin was so large, we didn't hear each other last night. I was okay with that. I walked over and gave CJ a hug and told him I was happy he was here.

We spent the rest of the day out on the Ross family's yacht. I thought I could really get used to this life. I just hoped Alex felt the same way.

Headed back to shore, I was sitting on Alex's lap with his arms wrapped around me, enjoying the setting sun. "I want to tell you something, but I'm worried I will scare you away," Alex said in a nervous voice.

I tried to turn around so I could reassure him, but he tightened his arms to keep me in place. "You're not going to scare me away, Alex."

"I'm falling in love with you," he said.

"That's good because I'm already in love with—"

Before I could finish the sentence, Alex flipped me around and kissed me passionately.

14

BRIDGET

Three Months Later

"Are you going to spend the whole day in there, or are you going to come out and work?" Patty asked. I really wanted to punch my assistant in the face. All I had done the whole week was hug the porcelain toilet, and it was starting to suck.

Alex kept calling me every five minutes to see if I was feeling better. *I just have the flu. Why can't these people leave me alone?*

"I will come out when I stop puking," I said through a vomit-filled mouth.

"If you weren't in denial, I would say you were pregnant. But we can keep playing like you have the flu if you want."

It hadn't even crossed my mind that I might be pregnant. I threw open the door and pulled Patty into the small bathroom. It didn't really fit two people very well. Patty's hair was colored pink and blue, and it made me smile.

In the last three months, Patty had grown closer to us. She had started to come over to my and Alex's condo and hang out with Sophie and me more often. I wished she would tell us about her past or let us into her life more. I hoped one day, she would feel comfortable letting us in.

"Patty, why are the bottom layers of your hair pink and the top ones blue? And why does your shirt say 'Who's The Daddy?'"

"Well, for the past week, all you've done is puke so much you've stopped drinking coffee. You have no other symptoms of the flu except you're always tired and cranky. The cranky part is normal you. The other two fall under the 'I'm Pregnant' category." The look she gave me said, "Don't try to deny it."

Then all the pieces started to fall into place. "Holy shit, I think I'm pregnant! What the fuck do I do?"

"Stop with the panic attack. I bought you three tests. I'm going to get you some water, and you are going to take the tests." *Wow. Patty's a good assistant. I hope I never lose her.*

"Patty, how did this happen?"

The look Patty gave me made me feel like an idiot. "You two fuck all the time—in your office, in your house, probably even in my office. When his thing goes into your vajayjay, little swimmy guys come out, and if you are not careful, you get a baby. Wow. Did you not go to school?" She threw her hands up and walked out the door, I guessed to get the water.

Come to think about it, that was a dumb question to ask. Who asks how a person gets pregnant? I wasn't going to ask Patty how I should tell Alex. She would try to get me to die my hair pink and blue, and that was not going to happen.

"Here you go," she said, coming back into the bathroom. "Now, start peeing on the stick, and let's see if I'm going to be an aunty." Ten minutes later, the tests read *pregnant*, two lines, and a plus sign. *I think I might be pregnant.*

"Now, get your ass up, brush your teeth, and go tell the Greek god he is going to be a daddy. Then go home and get some, because once that bundle of joy comes, your sex life is going to go out the door."

I drove across town in a daze. Time went by so fast, I didn't remember how I'd made it to Alex's office. I took the long elevator ride to the top floor. *Why do the executives always have to be on the top floor? Wouldn't it be easier to be on the second floor and make the underlings go up and up and up?*

Finally, after what felt like an hour, the elevator opened. I was armed with all three tests and a brand new one in case Alex needed me to make sure. I was starting to get excited. I was making a mini Alex. The baby would be beautiful. I couldn't wait to let Alex know.

In the last three months, we had expressed how much we meant to each other. I was living in Alex's penthouse and would be selling my house in the next few months. Everything was moving in the right direction. I would have never thought Alex would fall for me or love me as much as he did. I felt so cherished when I was in his arms and hoped nothing ever changed that.

Walking through the executive reception area, I noticed Sarah wasn't at her desk. So I walked toward Alex's office and heard him talking to Asher.

"I couldn't see myself having kids with her. It was a fling, and she should have known that going in."

That was all I heard of the conversation because my ears started to ring. The air seemed to disappear from my lungs, and tears ran down my face. I walked back toward the stairs because I didn't want to run into anyone on the elevator. I never wanted to see Alex again. My baby and I would make it on our own. I felt as though my heart was being ripped out of my chest. All I had wanted was someone to love and spend the rest of my life with.

Asher and Alex thought it was a joke that I didn't understand we were having a fling. I loved Alex with every fiber of my being, and he threw us in the trash like I was another one of his conquests. Walking down the stairs, so caught up in my drama, I didn't hear the door open or the man coming up behind me.

Everything went black. I had lost my forever man, and I might have been about to lose my life. But all I wanted now was to protect the little one growing in my belly.

15

ALEX

"So when are you going to ask Bridget to get married? You guys are with each other all the time. She pretty much lives with you." Asher had stopped over to give me an update on the Davis case. I was not happy about the update at all. I would need to let Bridget know what was going on when I got home tonight.

"If it were up to me, we would go to the courthouse and get married today. She's been sick for the last few days, which has me worried because I had planned to fly her to Vail this weekend and ask her at the winter house. That house has the best view. I thought I would ask her at sunset on the deck overlooking the mountains."

Asher was quiet for a minute, and then what he said surprised me. "I'm happy you waited. I think Bridget is perfect for our family. I thought you would have married Stacey."

Stacey was my last long relationship, maybe a week long, but we had been seen out together often since then. "I couldn't see myself having kids with her. It was a fling, and she should have known that going in. We'd take each other to social events when we didn't have other dates."

The feelings I had for Bridget were so much more than I could ever explain. If anything ever happened to her, I didn't know how I would live with myself. She was my everything, and I didn't care how sappy that made me sound.

"Enough about me. How are you and CJ doing?" Those two had been inseparable since Bridget had introduced them. It was nice seeing Asher happy.

The smile that spread across his face when he talked about his partner was amazing. "We're doing good. I think we're going to sell his house, and he's going to move in with me permanently. We've been going to Sam's BDSM club, Sanctorum, and taking classes. We both enjoy it, and it has brought a new dynamic to our relationship."

Asher and I were still talking when Antonio came storming into my office with a panicked look on his face. "We have a major issue. Bridget has been kidnapped by Mr. Davis, and we lost the tail on him." *Did my brother just say he lost the love of my life?*

CJ, Sophie, and Patty came running into my office next. They all looked as though they might lose it. Patty's hair was colored pink and blue, and her shirt said something about daddies. If this weren't such a dire situation, I might have asked if she was pregnant.

"When was the last time anyone saw her?" Asher asked.

"She left our office an hour ago to come speak to Alex," Patty replied with a strange look on her face.

"I didn't see her."

Antonio nodded. "We pulled up camera footage of the building. She ran out of your reception area, crying. She went down the stairwell, and then in the next sighting, she's with Mr. Davis, speeding out of the loading dock area in his van."

Why was she crying? Before I had time to think about it, Patty drop-kicked me in the stomach, flipped me on my back, and was yelling at me. Antonio grabbed her from behind and held her while I tried to get myself under control.

"What the fuck is wrong with you, Patty?" I didn't have time for this. Bridget had been kidnapped.

Patty had tears running down her face. "How could you do this to her? Why would you turn her away on the happiest day of your lives?"

"I don't understand what you are talking about? I haven't seen Bridget since this morning."

"She didn't talk to you before she ran out of your office, crying?" Patty was yelling and looked a little pale.

"I already said I haven't seen her since this morning. Why would you think I would make her cry?" I yelled back.

"Umm, we need to find Bridget fast." Everyone turned to Patty. She knew something she wasn't telling us.

I was ten seconds away from losing it when Asher rounded on Patty. "We are going to find her, but you know something else, so tell us what's going on." Asher was using his military voice, which was known to make women cry.

"Stop being an ass, Asher. Patty, come here and tell us what is going on." CJ took Patty into a hug.

"I can't tell you. It's not my place," Patty whispered.

"You have to tell us, now."

Patty whispered something into CJ's ear that made him go pale.

"What the fuck is going on? Tell me now!" I screamed at the people in the room.

CJ looked me straight and the eye and told me I was going to be a dad. The situation went from fucked up to "Holy shit, someone is going to die for touching my future wife and kid."

16

BRIDGET

Slowly, I felt as if I were coming out of the clouds. My tongue felt like the Syrian Desert. *What the fuck happened?* I tried to remember everything. I had a bun in the oven. Alex ripped my heart out of my chest. Every part of my body hurt. My hands were tied together with rope. I was pretty sure being tied up was not in my favor.

"I know you're awake. Open your eyes, you little bitch." I knew that voice. *What the fuck is he doing out of jail, and why do my eyelids feel so heavy?*

I needed to see if I had my phone on me. If I did, CJ, Patty, or Sophie could ping my phone when they realized I was missing. I hoped they would figure it out quickly because I wouldn't last long. I needed to protect the little one. I had taken a few classes from Asher in self-defense. But my hands were tied together. We hadn't gotten to the classes yet about what to do if you were tied up. Since I'd now been tied up twice, maybe we needed to move that class up on the schedule.

"Stop acting like you're not awake..." I didn't hear everything he had to say because he kicked my side. I needed to protect my little peanut. *It's you, me, and the hackers at work, little one. We can get through this.*

"What do you want, Mr. Davis? Why are you trying to kill me again? Why not go after Alex?" I really didn't want him to go after Alex, even if the ogre ripped out my heart.

"You have what we need."

"I'm sorry. We? Do you have an imaginary friend with you?"

He grabbed the back of my head and dragged me across the disgustingly dirty floor to a laptop. *Why don't kidnappers ever have clean accommodations? They always want something out of the kidnappee. Why not at least give us a clean working surface? And could the dumbass not bring the laptop to me?*

Once deposited in front of the laptop, I took stock of my location. The room smelled like someone had left dead fish carcasses out in the sun for a few days. There were no overhead lights, just a candle lighting the room. *Really? He couldn't have picked a location with working lights?*

"We, as in your father and I. We need you to pull up his old servers." So this was about the data I stole and locked down good so no one would get to it.

I wasn't sure how I wanted to play this out. If I gave Mr. Davis the data, he would fuck over a lot of people and probably kill me. If I didn't give him the data, he would definitely kill me. This was a "damned if you do and damned if you don't" situation.

Why can't my white knight ride in and save me? Oh, that's right. I don't have a white knight. He thinks we entered into this relationship, knowing there was an end date. I didn't get the memo about that, and I'm still pissed. I'm not sure how I'm going to seek my revenge. Can you seek revenge on your baby's daddy?

I thought I would try stalling to give my friends time to find me. "That will take me hours to get back." It wouldn't, really. I could have it pulled up in ten seconds. But I was going to make it take six hours. Hackers or computer nerds could take the long route to retrieve data, but it really took no time at all. We just needed to make our jobs look hard, or everyone would have been learning to hack. We were protecting the world.

Mr. Davis pointed to the laptop, and I started to type. If only he knew I was also sending CJ a code in the background. *Don't ever kidnap a hacker and then give them a laptop.*

Alex

"What do you mean her signal dropped and you can't find her?" I was ready to kill someone. The only problem was I needed all the people in this room.

CJ looked at me like I was stupid. I understood what he'd said. I just hadn't liked it. Then his cell made a pinging noise. CJ looked down, and a large smile appeared on his face. "We can work with this. Sophie, grab a laptop. We need to get to work."

I was getting angrier by the minute. "You want to tell me what you can work with?"

Asher looked over CJ's shoulder. "What's going on?"

"Bridget just sent a message about needing help. Psycho kidnapped her and is trying to get her to pull old server stuff."

CJ's fingers were flying across the keyboard, and different screens were flashing by. None of it made sense, and no one was saying anything, which was really starting to piss me off.

"Where is Bridget?"

CJ huffed and held up a finger, telling me he needed a minute. Two minutes later, he turned the laptop toward me and said, "Right here."

I wanted to kiss CJ, even though I didn't swing that way.

"Let's go." I was grabbing my keys when Asher put his hand on my shoulder to stop me. "If you think for one second I'm not going with, you've lost your ever-fucking mind."

Antonio was the one who jumped to my aid. "You can go, but you stay in the SUV until we bring her out. We don't need any of this 'let's save the day' shit."

I could live with that, hopefully.

I jumped in the SUV with CJ, Alex, and Asher. We sent Patty and Sophie back to the White Hat Security office. We didn't need more people getting hurt. Neither woman was happy about this. I told them to come over first thing tomorrow so they could see Bridget.

We got to the warehouse on the other side of town faster than I thought we would. Sam and a couple of his employees were already there. He gave us a report of the intel they had gathered while waiting for us to arrive. "We looked around. The good thing is he's alone. The bad thing is he has a gun pointed at her."

Asher, Antonio, and Sam came up with a game plan. They went in with their men, while CJ and I stood outside. It was the longest ten minutes of my life. I wasn't even sure what CJ and I talked about. All I wanted was my little nerd back.

Finally, I saw her walking out. I didn't wait for the all

clear. I ran up, grabbed her, and pulled her into my arms. She started hitting me and cussing at me. *What the fuck did I do?*

"Let me go, you asshole. Why are you even here? I heard you say I was a fling. Leave me the fuck alone." Now things were starting to become clear. Bridget must have heard only part of my talk with Asher. That was why she took off crying.

"You are not a fling. You are the love of my life, and we need to have a doctor check over you and the baby."

Bridget went still. "We want nothing to do with you."

"Stop lying. It's only going to get you into more trouble. You're already in trouble for eavesdropping. You didn't catch the whole conversation. I wasn't talking about you. I was talking about a past relationship and how it doesn't compare to you."

"Oh."

"That's all? Oh?"

She looked up at me with her crooked glasses and messed up hair and said, "Pregnancy hormones make you do crazy things."

I couldn't wait to spend the rest of my life with this woman.

The next hour was spent letting the paramedic look at Bridget and talking to the police. This time, Mr. Davis didn't make it out of the building alive. I didn't ask how. I let Sam, Asher, and Antonio explain that to the police.

There was a lot of tension in the elevator on the ride up to my condo. I wanted Bridget so bad. The mixture of almost losing her and knowing she was the woman carrying my baby was intense.

17

BRIDGET

Alex pushed me up against the elevator wall. "We can't do this here. Alex, we need to stop," I said weakly.

Over the past few months, we'd had some good make-out sessions followed by some unbelievable sex. The way Alex was kissing me now was nothing close to what had come before. I was faintly aware of the elevator coming to a stop and Alex carrying me into the penthouse.

When Alex said I had heard him wrong, I'd wanted him that second. The only thing that had stopped me was the people all around us.

Thankfully, Asher and Antonio were going to clean everything up with the police. They said they were going to come over tomorrow to tell me what steps I had to take next. We needed to get more information on my father. I needed to go to the police station and let them know everything that was said.

Even though I half-heartedly asked Alex to stop, he had a different idea. He'd had his hands all over me since the elevator ride, and I certainly wasn't going to complain. Between kisses, he finally said, "I don't want to stop. Ever since I saw you walk out of that place, all I can think about is being inside you to make sure you are real and nothing happened to you."

No matter how many times Alex and I made love, it felt like the first time. His words always brought a rush of excitement. Slowly, Alex kissed down the nape of my neck, while his fingers worked to pull off the scrub top the paramedics had given me.

"You're not wearing a bra?" Alex asked with a groan while dragging his finger down my collarbone to circle my nipple and lightly tug it. Alex's eyes were dilated with passion. I could feel his dick rubbing against me through his dress pants.

"No," I said tenderly.

"Fuck," Alex swore quietly in my ear.

"Well, if you would hurry and move this to the bedroom, we could." *Come on. I'm a horny pregnant lady, and you're killing me with foreplay.*

Alex swung me over his shoulder with my ass in the air and took off toward our bedroom. "I need to get you into our bed so I can feast on you properly." Then I was flying through the air, and my body bounced on the bed.

Without taking his eyes off me, Alex crawled onto the bed and started kissing his way down my body, stopping to suck on each of my nipples, making my clit start to throb.

"Alex, please," I moaned, not sure what I wanted him to do. He continued to suck and pull at my nipples, then he slowly moved his mouth and hands down my body, kissing me, until he got to my stomach.

He worked on removing my pants, slowly ran his index finger along my slit, and lowered his mouth to my clit. The pleasure of his mouth on my clit and his fingers in me lasted only a few minutes before I had an orgasm.

"Alex, I want to suck on you," I said after coming out of my orgasm-induced haze.

"I'm too wound up to have those lips on me. Wrap your legs around me instead." Alex hurried to take off his clothes and climbed back on top of me.

I wrapped my legs around his waist. I wanted Alex inside of me more than anything I could think of. I could feel myself getting wetter as I anticipated his entrance.

Alex put two fingers inside me again to make sure I was still ready. "Damn. You are so wet and eager for me. That turns me on so much." Alex pulled his fingers from me, and the emptiness made me whimper until I could feel his cock press against me. When he pushed inside, it was pure bliss.

Alex took me slow and easy at first. I fell into a happy slumber after our lovemaking. He woke me up an hour later and took me hard and fast. "I needed that," Alex said when we were done.

We lay there for minutes, maybe hours, listening to each other breathe. When Alex finally broke the silence, I knew we had to talk about what had happened. That didn't mean I wanted to.

"I've never been more scared in my life than when I found out you were kidnapped. Then Patty told us you were pregnant. I didn't know what to do, and I was so worried I was going to lose you," Alex said to me while trailing his hands up and down my spine.

"Honestly, I was so mad at you for what you said, I wanted to get away from Mr. Davis just so I could take revenge on you."

"Bridget, I want to spend the rest of my life with you," Alex told me.

"I want to spend my life with you and this little nugget," I replied, rubbing my stomach.

Alex leaped out of bed and grabbed something off the dresser. When he came back, he knelt next to the bed. "I wanted to wait until this weekend and do this right at the house in Vale. But I can't wait any longer. Bridget, I love you with every fiber of my being. Will you marry me?"

"You have a house in Vale?"

"Really, you're going to leave me hanging?"

"Of course, I will marry you, but I think we should still go to that house this weekend and celebrate."

EPILOGUE

PATTY

Bridget looked like a princess straight out of a fairytale in her Vera Wang vintage wedding dress and slight baby bump. The whole crew was at the Waldorf for Alex and Bridget's wedding. The exchange of vows was unbelievable and didn't leave a dry eye in the audience.

Like always, I sneaked in the back and tried to stay under the radar. There was too much press coverage at this wedding. I couldn't afford for my identity to get out. When Bridget asked me to be in her wedding, it was the hardest day of my life. I said one day I would tell her the story, but until then, I couldn't let the media get ahold of my picture.

The reception was on another level. Bridget had left the whole reception up to Alex's parents to plan. All she wanted was to marry Alex. The Ross family did not leave anything on the table. Pink crystals hung from the ceiling. White lights twinkled around the room. Watching all the people dancing on the floor brought tears to my eyes. All of these people getting to live their lives how they wanted was unfair. I was feeling sorry for myself.

Bridget was five months pregnant and glowed with

happiness. I noticed Alex's dad was also bragging about getting his first grandbaby, saying it was all because of him.

On the other side of the room, I saw my sister and her husband arguing once again. Most people would look at them and think they were having an intense conversation. I could tell from my sister's face that it was an argument. We were twins. I could almost sense it.

No one knew we were twins or that we even knew each other. If I stood next to my sister, it might have been obvious. We had to keep our identities undercover, or we would lose what life we had. We had agreed that as long as our identities stayed hidden, we could live in the United States. The second our identities were leaked, we would need to move to my father's home country.

That wasn't going to stop me from bringing down her husband. He was a lowlife piece of shit, and I would get the information I needed so she could have a clean divorce. I would start that project very soon.

In the meantime, I enjoyed the flow of the music and watched people live their lives as if nothing was ever going to change for them. I would have loved to get to know the handsome groomsman named Sam. I overheard the women behind me talking about him. Maybe I would look into him and see if I could trust him enough to have a fling.

I had to be careful who we brought into our lives. First thing tomorrow, I was going to hack my sister's husband's accounts and figure out where he was going. Bridget might have thought I was some dumb receptionist, but what she didn't know was I owned Black Hat, the top IT firm in the country. Since I couldn't have my picture shown anywhere, I had top executives who reported to me.

All anyone knew was that the Royal Hacker owned the

company. What they didn't know was who he was. But it wasn't a he; it was me.

The End

ROYAL HACKER the second novel in the White Hat Security, series is now available. Royal Hacker Store Link

AUTHOR NOTE'S

White Hat Security Series

Hacker Exposed

Royal Hacker

Misunderstood Hacker

Undercover Hacker

Hacker Revelation

Hacker Christmas

Hacker Salvation - June 11, 2019

Immortal Dragon

The Dragon's Psychic - July 9, 2019

The Dragon's Human - 2019

Montana Gold (Brotherhood Kindle World)

Grayson's Angel

Noah's Love

Bryson's Treasure - 2019

A Flipping Love Story (Badge of Honor World)

Unlocking Dreams

Unlocking Hope - 2019

Siblings of the Underworld

Hell's Key (Part of the Shadows and Sorcery Box Set) May 28, 2019

Visit linzibaxter.com for more information and release dates.
Join Linzi Baxter Newsletter at Newsletter

PLEASE LEAVE A REVIEW!

If you enjoyed this book, I would appreciate your help so other can enjoy it, too.

Review it. Please tell other readers why you liked this book by reviewing it at amazon.com. Thank you!

Recommend it. Please help other readers find this book by recommending it to friends, readers' groups and discussion boards.

ABOUT THE AUTHOR

Linzi Baxter hails from Bismarck, North Dakota, but currently lives in Orlando, Florida. She received her bachelor's degree in information technology from the University of Central Florida and is currently in the process of earning her MBA from the same university.

Linzi works as an IT manager for the local government and spends her free time playing with her basset hound, watching college sports, traveling to Europe's great cities, and reading romance. It was that last passion that inspired her to write her debut novella, *Hacker Exposed*.